GUN LEVELED, HE YANKED THE DOOR OPEN . . .

She stood there in gossamer, her raven-black hair brushed across her shoulders. The thin light bled through the flimsy white nightgown and outlined her magnificent body.

"You won't need that," Sophia said, nodding toward his gun. Her eyes swept over his naked body and a smile turned up the corners of her full mouth. "I would like to come in," she said, and Ruff backed into the room. She followed him, silently closing and latching the door.

"Did I disturb you?" Sophia murmured as she pressed against him and her lips sought his.

"You are," Ruff said, kissing the nape of her neck and letting his mouth slide along the smooth, scented flesh while his fingers untied the two bows which fastened the bodice of her nightgown.

"You said you never mixed business and bed," she reminded him.

"I promise not to think of business once. . . ."

RUFF JUSTICE #3

Blood on the Moon

by

Warren T. Longtree

A SIGNET BOOK
NEW AMERICAN LIBRARY
TIMES MIRROR

PUBLISHER'S NOTE

This novel is a work of fiction. Names, characters, places, and incidents are either the product of the author's imagination or are used fictitiously, and any resemblance to actual persons, living or dead, events, or locales is entirely coincidental.

NAL BOOKS ARE AVAILABLE AT QUANTITY DISCOUNTS
WHEN USED TO PROMOTE PRODUCTS OR SERVICES. FOR
INFORMATION PLEASE WRITE TO PREMIUM MARKETING DIVISION,
THE NEW AMERICAN LIBRARY, INC., 1633 BROADWAY,
NEW YORK, NEW YORK 10019.

The first chapter of this book appeared in *Night of the Apache*, the second volume of this series.

SIGNET TRADEMARK REG. U.S. PAT. OFF. AND FOREIGN COUNTRIES
REGISTERED TRADEMARK—MARCA REGISTRADA
HECHO EN CHICAGO, U.S.A.

SIGNET, SIGNET CLASSICS, MENTOR, PLUME, MERIDIAN AND NAL
BOOKS are published by The New American Library, Inc.,
1633 Broadway, New York, New York 10019

First Printing, December, 1981

1 2 3 4 5 6 7 8 9

PRINTED IN THE UNITED STATES OF AMERICA

1

SHE WAS WARM beside him, and the morning sunlight through the curtains painted wavering highlights across her dark, silky hair, and so at the first knock on his door Justice simply let his hand continue its interesting journey along the swell of her thigh, ignoring the uncivil interruption.

At the second knock Sue Lin's head lifted curiously, but he whispered, "Ignore it, they'll go away," and she did so, snuggling up against him, her leg thrown up over his thigh.

The knocking at the door became more insistent, and a man's voice boomed:

"Open up, Justice. We know you're in there!"

"They know I'm in here," he whispered, kissing the tip of Sue Lin's nose. She giggled, and her hand crept up his leg like a fleshy tarantula.

"Justice!"

"And I thought San Franciscans were remarkable for

their hospitality," Justice said. "You certainly have been."

Sue Lin giggled again and shifted beneath the sheet. She laughed in all of the right places, Justice observed, which was very good indeed for a woman who had no English at all. Perhaps she thought all of his utterances quite profound or sublimely humorous. The best of company, he considered. He held her tightly, and sighed with irritation as the pounding on the door continued.

"All right, you know I'm in here!" he shouted. "I know you're out there. Now go away!"

It was silent, and he turned to Sue Lin. Then someone put a foot to the door and it slammed open, splintering away from the latch. Sue Lin leaped from the bed and ran naked across the room and between the two big-shouldered men, leaving Justice with only a last memorable glimpse of her superb honey-colored buttocks.

"You can't imagine how annoying that is," Justice said calmly.

A third man had appeared in the doorway, and his face was dark, savagely intelligent. Or perhaps it just appeared so as he stood between the two huge, dumb-looking brutes with him.

"Now get up out of that sack, Justice. The Baroness Sophia wants to see you."

"Oh?" He raised an eyebrow. "Give her my regrets."

The dark man took a step forward, studying Justice. He didn't look that tough, he decided. Tall—that was apparent even lying down as he was now—with long dark hair as fine and curled as a woman's. Justice wore a long mustache which drooped past his jawline. He had icy blue eyes and a slender nose. He looked rangy, but wasn't swollen with muscle. His chest was pale, his neck and face burned with the wind and the weather.

Gorman Mix decided he could take Justice at any

game. He turned to the big man beside him. "Yank him out of that bed, Hurly."

Hurly nodded and with dark enthusiasm stepped to the foot of the bed. "Ya heard 'im," Hurly said in a voice so deep and slow it seemed hardly human.

"I heard him. Hurly, I didn't like being disturbed. I don't know who in hell you men are, what you want. But you have made me angry, Hurly. I'm not getting up. Get your tails out of this room."

Hurly made a low growling sound. Laughter, threat, disgust—Justice could not tell which. But the big man moved forward, lowered his shotgun, and stretched out a hand to yank the sheet from Justice.

The gun exploded, the noise deafening. The room filled with a haze of black-powder smoke, and Hurly was slammed backward as if he had been kicked by a mule.

He snatched at his shoulder and sat down, pawing at the hole torn through the meat and bone. He looked at Justice and toppled over.

Gorman Mix, who had been moving forward as well, halted dead. Justice's face was expressionless. The hole in the bed sheet still smoldered, and Justice turned those icy blue eyes on Mix, slightly shifting the pistol under his sheet.

"Please leave now. And take your friend with you."

Mix nodded slowly, his eyes burning with suppressed anger. The other big man stood over Hurly. He snuffled and wiped his eyes. Justice half expected him to get down on all fours and sniff the injured Hurly like a surprised, confused animal. He was obviously Hurly's brother, no smarter and only half a head shorter.

"You had a gun. In bed," he mumbled as if Justice had not been playing fair.

"A barbaric habit of mine," Ruff said mildly. "Now

get out of here. Even in San Francisco it's against the law to break into a hotel room and threaten a man."

The gunshot had been audible all over the hotel. Justice heard the rush of feet in the hallway, and a balding, slight man peered in and then backed out. Mix and the big man hoisted a moaning Hurly to his feet. His side was painted with blood, his face distorted with pain.

"The Baroness'll . . ." Mix began.

"I'll speak for myself, Mr. Mix."

Justice glanced to the doorway to see a woman in black. She wore black lace gloves to her elbows, a black satin dress, and a tiny black hat with a veil which was turned up and away from her pale, pale face.

"Baroness!"

"See to your thug, Mr. Mix. I'll speak to Mr. Justice personally."

"What's happened?" The desk clerk, a redheaded man with no chin at all and the reddest complexion Justice had ever seen, peered into the room. He looked from Justice to Hurly to the Baroness and back, gasping at each figure. "I'll get the police!"

"No!" the Baroness said hurriedly, sticking out a restraining hand.

"It's all right," Justice drawled. "I was showing Hurly my gun and it went off."

Unconvinced, the clerk looked at Hurly, who muttered that he was all right. The clerk frowned at Justice, who was actually smiling, and then at the splintered doorframe.

"Charge that door to the Baroness," Justice said.

"Yes," she agreed hastily. "I'll pay for that."

The clerk believed none of it, but if they were satisfied and the damages would be taken care of, he was only too happy to get clear of them. With a quick bow he departed, and they could hear him shooing off the bystanders in the hall.

Hurly was leaning on his brother's arm, his face ashen. Mix lingered in the room, and the Baroness had to tell him again, "Go on now. I'll be all right."

"Ma'am . . ."

"*Now*, Mr. Mix," she said sharply, and he nodded meekly.

"Yes, ma'am."

They went out, shutting the shattered door behind them, and the Baroness calmly unpinned her hat, placing it on the bureau with her gloves. She stopped to pat her hair and then turned to Justice, who had been coolly observing her all this time.

Tall, with high, full breasts, she had black eyes which gazed with amusement from an ivory-white face. That combination made Justice think of Spain, but she didn't strike him as being Spanish. She had a narrow waist which flared into wide, compelling hips, and she moved with a grace which accentuated them.

Her face was perfectly, delicately formed, with full lips and a straight, almost long nose. Yet there was a rigidity about that face it was almost as if she wore a cunningly contrived mask, and perhaps that's what it was—the mask that strict training and fine breeding sometimes stretches over an aristocrat's face. Justice had known some aristocratic ladies in his time, and they all had had that reserve, that aloofness.

Yet it could be mocked, and in his short time in San Francisco, he had encountered more than one lady who used a title she was not entitled to.

"I apologize for my employees' behavior," she said suddenly, with a quick smile and a limp gesture of those white, long-fingered hands. "They are overzealous at times."

She looked at the tall man who lay covered only by a sheet and smiled again, briefly. It was a practiced, elegant smile, likely turned on anyone in her proximity, but there was a coolness which lingered after the smile had passed.

"Fine," Ruff said. "Now would *you* mind getting out, Baroness?"

She blinked as if she was not used to being spoken to in that way. She opened her mouth to speak, but Justice went on:

"Your intrusion has disturbed me, Baroness. Disturbed me greatly."

"Yes, I saw her leave," she said dryly.

"Now will you do the same?"

"I'm here on business," she said, waving a condescending hand.

"Business? I don't conduct business in bed."

"Is this your advertisement?" she asked, drawing a newspaper clipping from her black handbag. He didn't have to look at it to see that it was. He had put it in the *Examiner* only yesterday. Well, he thought with faint amusement, they did promise quick results.

" 'Guide, woodsman, rough-country scout for hire,' " she read.

"I know what the advertisement says," Ruff interrupted.

" 'Army experience, available for exploration, travel, game hunting. Contact Ruffin T. Justice, St. Regis Hotel.' " She finished and folded the clipping away, looking up expectantly when she was finished.

"I need you, Mr. Justice."

"Baroness, I don't want to work for you, in any capacity."

"I'm willing to pay you handsomely," she insisted.

"It's not the money . . ."

"No? I think it is. Why else advertise? 'Army experience,' your advertisement said. Why are you no longer with the army, Mr. Justice?"

"None of your damned business, ma'am," he said flatly.

"Nevertheless," she said, walking to where her hat and gloves lay, "I wish to hire you, and you will find the money extraordinary. I want to repay you for what our intrusion might have cost you—in every way," she added without an expression Justice could read.

"Since you do not mix business and bed, please meet me in the dining room in fifteen minutes. We shall go over the details. Goodbye." She flitted out of the room, leaving Justice alone in the hotel bed, where still the acrid scent of gunpowder lingered.

He lay there a long while, watching the shadows shift before the sunlight through the curtains. Then reluctantly he rose.

Naked, with his pistol still in his right hand, Justice walked to the basin which was set into the wall of the paneled alcove. The St. Regis boasted a modern marvel—water was piped into each room from a cistern on the roof of the hotel. Ruff turned the spigot and watched as the water ran down the drain.

Wearily he lifted his eyes to his mirror image and half smiled. Then he closed his eyes and rinsed his face and upper torso. That done, he brushed his long black hair and returned to the bedroom to dress.

He was puzzled, upset and mystified at once by the morning's intrusion. When the lady wanted to hire somebody she didn't hem and haw around. Batter the door down and yank them from their beds.

He dressed in his dark city suit and ruffled shirt. He tied a black string tie around his neck and dabbed on some of the cologne Corinne had bought for him uptown. Come to think of it, she had paid for the suit as well. But he had earned the gifts; she saw to that.

He frowned at his mirror image. "You look citified again, Mr. Justice."

It was as bad as Paris when he had gone over the second time with Bill Cody. Bright lights and dancing, fancy women and fine brandy. Ruff had an urge for that life, a need for it, it seemed, by the way he kept returning to it. Yet he was restless again, as he had always grown restless, feeling restricted, only two-thirds a man as he prowled the brick roads and gaslighted ballrooms.

It came to him suddenly at times. He would see a down-at-the-heels prospector, smelling of leather and tobacco, hides, powder, and sage, and Justice's heart would start pumping with excitement.

He knew what it was. For a long while he had pretended not to know, since it revealed some sort of major flaw in Ruffin T. Justice's makeup. But he knew.

It was the danger. War and hard weather; walking the high-country ridges or standing with a Colt in either hand while the arrows flew past his head. He loved it, craved it, needed it.

"You are a savage, Mr. Justice," he told the dandy in the mirror, and the mirror image winked back with a quick, knowing smile.

He wore a shoulder holster just now. It hardly rumpled the lines of his suit. He preferred a long-barreled Peacemaker, a gun with enough thump to put down whatever you hit, but in town he carried a neat little Colt New Line Pocket .41 with a two-and-a-quarter-inch barrel.

Downstairs he crossed the deep-red carpet under brass chandeliers, which burned with the blue flame of gas, and entered the hotel dining room.

He saw her immediately, across the room. She sat in shadow and muted light, her eyes on him. She was a proud, beautiful creature, and Justice did not trust her for a minute.

But he crossed the dining room, knowing he would hear her out, knowing that if the job was right he would work for this cold and aloof woman; and he was not sure even now if it was the danger which was calling him, the promise of gold, or the lure of a beautiful woman.

2

THE BARONESS WATCHED with sparkling eyes as he approached her table in the corner of the hotel dining room. Somehow she had found the time to change her clothes, and she now wore a white satin dress, the neckline plunging revealingly. It was a dress calculated to distract a man, Ruff thought.

She was alone, or appeared to be. Without seeming to, Justice glanced around the gilt and crystal, the silver and crimson of the dining room, and he saw the straight-backed, dark-haired man sitting alone at a table across the room from the Baroness.

He was studying his menu innocuously, assiduously, but Ruff caught his single swift glance and let his own eyes slide away. He had the feeling that this woman was never truly alone.

"I'm so glad you decided to meet with me, Mr. Justice," the Baroness said as Ruff seated himself.

"Yes, and isn't this much nicer than having me bound and thrown into your room?"

"Gorman Mix has . . . different ways of doing things," she said. A slightly pained expression followed her brief smile. "At times I'm sorry I hired him. But he was available, and I knew no one in this country. Can we please forget all of that and come to business?"

"All right. I only want you forewarned that my services do not come cheap," Ruff said.

"I wouldn't expect them to." Her eyes swept over him. She turned her glass of brandy in her white, ringed hands. "But I would expect excellence from you, Mr. Justice."

"Just what sort of problem do you have, Baroness? I can't see you tramping through the woods after bear. I assume it's not a hunting party you're trying to organize."

"No." She hesitated and, Ruff noticed, glanced to the man at the table across the way. "Will you have a drink, Mr. Justice?"

"No. I don't drink."

"No?" She lifted a surprised eyebrow. It hung delicately arched over her dark, glittering eye. "Unusual in this part of the world, isn't it?"

"I suppose. At least I don't have to worry about missing it when I'm on the trail. The same goes for tobacco."

"And the women?" she asked brazenly.

"Women are not a vice," Ruff said with a smile.

"Obviously you have not met any of my friends, then."

"Did we come here to discuss my character?" Ruff prodded.

"No." Again her eyes shuttled to the dark man across the way. "All right." She sighed. "I've decided I want you to help me." Ruff nodded curiously, and she went on, first fortifying herself with a sip of amber-colored brandy.

"My title is no sham, Mr. Justice. I assure you we are an ancient and powerful family. My full name is the Baroness Sophia Mancek." She paused. "It means nothing to you?"

"No," he admitted, and she shrugged in disbelief.

"So empty is reputation," she said to herself. "Anyway, to go on . . ." She squared her shoulders. "My father is quite ill, Mr. Justice. Otherwise I would be quite satisfied to let the little fool lose herself in the wilderness—"

"I'm sorry," Ruff interrupted. "You're getting ahead of me."

"Of course, you wouldn't know. In Europe, of course, it is all the gossip."

"Of course," he replied, glancing at the far table. The man was gone.

"My younger sister, Lita, has disappeared in the wilderness of America, Mr. Justice. A place called Colorado. Near . . . Leadville?"

"Leadville, yes. I know the area." Ruff halted Sophia there. "She disappeared. Was she traveling?"

"Traveling! The little hoyden was tramping about on a hunting safari, you know? A baroness in breeches, climbing around the mountains. Well, she's long overdue."

"Baroness, I want to know exactly what is going on. Or what you suspect. Is there blackmail involved here? A kidnapping? What?"

"I don't know," she said. She was lying and Ruff knew it. He shrugged.

"Haven't you spoken to the authorities?" he asked. "The local sheriff, the federal marshal?"

"I can't . . ." Her voice trailed off, and she looked away.

"I don't see how I can help you," Ruff said, starting to rise. "Not if you won't tell me what's going on."

"All right!" the Baroness said so loudly that heads turned. Ruff sat down again. "She's run off with some barbarian of a mountain man. All very bucolic and romantic. To live in the hills with a buckskin-clad trapper she's left a life of luxury and glamour."

"Some people prefer one, some the other." Ruff asked her directly, "So you've come to haul her back?"

"As I've said, I couldn't care less how Lita throws away her life, but Father has asked for her. He hasn't long, Mr. Justice. Lita should at least be informed and given the choice."

"Seems to me she's made her choice," Ruff said. "This mountain man—what's his name?"

"Cody MacCormack. Do you know him?"

"No, but he's got a reputation. He's a fighter and a man who can live off the land in the high country, winter or summer. He's also known as an honest man. The Utes trust him like they trust no other white."

"You speak of him with respect yourself." Again the Baroness arched an eyebrow. Her full mouth pouted slightly as if the thought was disagreeable.

"I respect any man who makes his way alone through the world and stands tall. I don't know him, but I guess maybe I could like Cody MacCormack if he's what they say he is."

"Could you find him?" the Baroness asked, leaning nearer so that the white satin gown revealed the soft beginnings of her full, nearly round breasts.

"Find him? That's where Lita is, with MacCormack?"

"Of course. They say he's in the 'high country,' whatever that means."

"It means what it says, Baroness. Rocky Mountain country. Treacherous, awesome, wild and absolute death to a man who doesn't know how to live in it. Winter's setting in, Baroness, and there'll be forty feet of snow in the high passes before it's done. It's a barren, winter-mad world up there."

"It hasn't snowed yet," she said confidently.

"It will. Soon and hard. Do you mean you want to get in and out before winter does settle? Find Lita and bring her out if she'll come?"

"Exactly, Mr. Justice. Are you the man for the job?"

"At what price?"

"Ten thousand dollars," she said, and even Ruff was jolted a little by her offer. Soldiers were making thirteen dollars a month, cowhands a dollar a day. The mayor of San Francisco pulled down just under two thousand a year. "You could live long and well on that amount, wouldn't you say?" she asked, and her smile was confident.

"Yes." Ruff was silent, thoughtful for a minute. He didn't trust this one, not for a minute. Yet he could not pass up the offer. He nodded and told her, "I'm in."

"Good!" She positively beamed. Leaning back, Sophia took a deep breath, and somehow, in that dress, it seemed an invitation. "The train will leave at four, then. Be ready."

"The train?"

"Of course. My private train—lent to me by a dear old friend, Charles Coldwell. Do you know him?"

"Of him. He owns the Great Western Railroad."

"Of course, darling," she purred. Now that business was aside, she seemed to soften perceptibly. The Baroness stretched out a hand and covered Ruff's with it. It was cool, soft, and she patted him lightly. "We'll take the train through to Colorado. It's quickest, by far the easiest. From there it will be up to you. I mean to sequester myself in Leadville's—what an abominable name for a hamlet—in Leadville's finest hotel and allow you to do what you are noted for, running around the hills like a savage until you find Lita for me."

They rose together, and Ruff asked her, "Has anyone told you that there is Indian trouble up that way?"

"Yes, something about that. Renegades, they called them. Some nasty man called Stone Eyes and his band of Utah Indians—"

"Utes," Ruff corrected.

"Yes, Utes." She waved a hand nonchalantly. "But, darling, I'm sure they will be a minimum of trouble to a man of your talents. Besides," she said with a smile which was very narrow and very sharp, "you didn't think I was paying you ten thousand dollars to act as an errand boy, did you?"

No, he didn't. He thought of it later in his room as he packed. To get into and out of that wild country with its peaks towering over fourteen thousand feet, the passes blocked with snow, crawling with renegade Utes, was an unenviable job. It could get even more ticklish if, having somehow located Lita Mancek in that wilderness, Mr. Cody MacCormack took exception to someone wanting to haul her away.

MacCormack was reported to be a giant of a man, a true mountain man who had lived in the wilderness since the Indians ambushed the wagon train his parents were with twenty years back. Cody MacCormack was good with a gun, hell on wheels with a knife, and the devil himself in a bare-handed fight, it was said.

He wondered if MacCormack wasn't the main reason the Baroness had settled on Ruff Justice as her man. A man planning to winter up with his woman can object some to intruders.

The air was cool off the Pacific Ocean as Ruff went uptown. Already fog curled up the low inlets, and already the day grew gray. The harbor itself was a virtual forest of masts; ships from every port in the world rode at anchor. San Francisco was booming.

He found the shop he wanted and went in, a little bell tinkling as he entered the dark store. The smell of leather and lye soap and baled jeans was heavy. The sign outside had read "49er Outfitters." 1849 was long gone, and so was the gold, but there was still a brisk trade in outfitting would-be prospectors.

Everything a man could need and then some lined the rough plank shelving—canteens, picks, shovels, hats and pans, a variety of tinned goods and dried fruits, rifles and saddles, mule packs. Ruff walked slowly, observantly, through the aisles, the owner, a hunched, ancient Chinese, watching him.

He selected a sheepskin coat, badgerskin gloves, three boxes of .44-40s and a new Henry repeating rifle. On top of that he threw two pairs of long underwear and six pairs of socks.

"Going to cold country, huh?" the Chinese asked with a smile and a bobbing head. Ruff answered with a nod. He thought at the last minute of a few extra items which might come in handy, paid for his purchases with one of the Baroness's mint-new double eagles, and went back out into the foggy San Francisco afternoon. From far off he heard the hooting of a train whistle, and he turned that way, bundle over his shoulder, rifle in his hand.

There was a police cordon around the siding where Charles Coldwell's private train rested. The engineer had a good head of steam up, but they were still taking on water.

There were four cars in all behind the tender: two gold-scrolled Pullmans, a freight car painted a deep green, and a red caboose. The first policeman Ruff reached stopped him.

"Who are you?" he asked in a thick Irish brogue.

"Ruffin T. Justice, sir. I'm with the party."

The policeman looked Ruff up and down from his alligator boots to his flat-brimmed black Stetson, noticing with a silent murmur the ruffles at the cuffs and down the front of his white shirt.

"What's the name, O'Brian?" a sergeant called from near the first passenger car.

"Justice!" the policeman called back, and the sergeant waved his arm.

Ruff stepped around the cop with a slight nod and strode to the train. Steam escaped in tiny gasps from the brakes, and the bell rang three times.

"You're the last one," the police sergeant advised him. "They've been holding the train for you."

Ruff stepped up onto the platform and tried the door to the Pullman. It was locked, and so he rapped on the door, which was of carved cedar with solid brass hinges and knob.

In a minute a man in a red tunic, black trousers, and gleaming black boots opened the door. He had his thin blond hair parted in the middle and slicked back. He wore an insignia of rank Ruff was unfamiliar with on his epaulettes.

"Ruffin Justice?" He pronounced it "Joostis," but Ruff admitted to being himself. "You are three minutes late. I am Captain Saranevo."

"Glad to meet you, sir." Ruff had the idea that soldiers under Saranevo didn't last long if they made a habit of being three minutes late.

"Leave your baggage if you like," Saranevo said, flaring his nostrils slightly at the sight of the sheepskin coat. "Someone will take it to your compartment."

"All right."

"Come," Saranevo said, crooking a finger.

This first car was a dining room and saloon. A well-stocked liquor cabinet sat to one side, running half the length of the car. Myriad bottles rested securely in channeled compartments behind glass enforced with brass wire. The walls were paneled in cedar, hung with brass lanterns. The windows were draped with blue velvet. There were six small tables and one long banquet table, all set with silver, all fastened securely with brass angles to the floor of the Pullman.

They passed through a door and into the kitchen which adjoined the dining compartment. A small, swarthy man with a huge mustache glanced up from his colander, and the captain pointedly ignored the cook. Obviously one didn't fraternize with the help in Captain Saranevo's army either.

They stepped out another door onto the platform and then through to the second car, where the sleeping compartments were located. Saranevo tapped the door of the second compartment and said, "This will be yours, although frankly I don't see why you're not with the other Americans in the last car."

"It is my charm," Ruff said without smiling. The captain sniffed again.

They passed through a door midway through the Pullman and entered a sort of parlor room. The room was alive with chatter, and Justice saw the Baroness across the room. She wore green silk, and her hair was piled high, dressed with a strand of pearls. She held a glass in her hand, as did most of the others. Gorman Mix and his thugs were excluded from this company, of course. They would be in the next car—that for the Americans, as Captain Saranevo had not so graciously put it. Ruff knew none of these people, except for one man, a tall, ramrod-straight American army colonel with a flowing silver mustache and hard, hard eyes.

The Baroness had Ruff's arm. Her eyes glittered—a part of that was due to liquor, Ruff guessed. "Darling," she gushed. "Do meet our companions."

She guided him through the room, which was furnished with twin gold-colored settees, a long mahogany table, and gold drapes.

"This is Vice-Premier Chapek," she said, introducing Ruff to a bulky man with a scar across his cheek. The big man shook hands stiffly, without closing his fingers. "And General Ankirat," she said, nodding to a completely bald man with a monocle. He held a drink balanced on his knee. His chest was spattered with pounds of medals. Gold rope dripped from the shoulder of his red uniform tunic.

"General," Ruff nodded. The old soldier lifted one finger in response.

"And Zardan," Sophia said, turning Ruff to face the dark man he had seen in the hotel dining room. Zardan, whatever his position or rank, dressed commonly in an ash-gray suit and narrow gray tie. His welcome was no warmer than anyone else's, but his interest was sharper. Perhaps he was some sort of secret service man, a bodyguard. At any rate, Zardan was obviously not the sort to take people at face value.

"And your fellow American," the Baroness said. She walked Ruff to where the colonel stood beside the Pullman's window. "Colonel Bryson Hargrove. Colonel, this is—"

"I know who the bastard is," Hargrove said coldly. His gray eyes locked with Ruff's for a long minute. Then he bowed quickly to the Baroness. "I apologize for my language and my manner, Baroness Mancek. But I will not remain in the same room with Ruffin T. Justice."

With that Hargrove put his drink down on the table and turned sharply toward the rear door of the parlor compartment. The Baroness's face was blank with surprise, Zardan smiled thinly, and General Ankirat muttered, "By God."

"Always nice to renew old acquaintances," Ruff said dryly.

"What was that about?" the Baroness asked. "I don't think I've ever seen an American officer lose his composure like that."

"I've seen him lose his composure. Often," Ruff said without explaining anything. "Just what is the colonel doing on your train, if I may ask, Baroness?"

"What?" She seemed hardly to have heard the question. She emerged from the fog of her private musings to answer him, "Colonel Hargrove is en route to Colorado to take over the garrison there, to take command of the forces opposing Stone Eyes."

"But why on this train?"

"Mr. Coldwell asked me to allow the colonel to accompany us. I had no objection, of course. Colonel Hargrove is most agreeable . . . up until now. I'm sorry, Mr. Justice, I seem to have brought old enemies together."

"No apology necessary," Ruff said. The train started forward with a lurch, and Ruff braced himself against the wall. A second lurch and a third, and then the train was rolling smoothly. Captain Saranevo, standing near the window, parted the gold-colored drapes, and Ruff looked out to see San Francisco's wharves sliding away, to catch a last glimpse of the colorful buildings in Chinatown, a last flash of Nob Hill and its mansions. Within minutes the train had switched off onto the western line and there were only scattered farms against deep-green fields and the first sketchings of mountain ranges against an iron-gray sky.

"I think we should all retire to our compartments," the Baroness suggested. "Dinner will be at five-thirty." Aside to Ruff she said, "I shall speak to the colonel. Whatever his grievance is against you, I won't have it aired on my train."

There was determination on her lovely face, and Ruff

bowed; he did not say what he was thinking—that nothing on God's earth could force Colonel Bryson Hargrove to be civil to Ruff Justice.

He returned to his compartment through the swaying corridor. His baggage had been brought in, and his clothing from the hotel was already hung in the closets. Ruffin locked the door and had a closer look. His white elkskin shirt hung next to his gray suit, and he removed it from the hanger. He laid it on his fold-down bed and examined it closely.

There was a small pocket in the front of the beaded shirt, and that pocket had been sealed shut with wax. Had been, because the seal was broken now, the wax crumbled down inside the pocket.

Whoever had hung these clothes had taken the time to search them. Ruff smiled thinly and hung the shirt again. Were they on to him?

He doubted it. Probably just a precaution. Yet he had a trainload of enemies, and everything would have to be done with the utmost caution.

Gorman Mix and his thugs were in the last car. Clive Colter would be glad of the chance to get even with the man who had shot Hurly. Zardan he did not trust at all. The man was a professional. And of course there was Colonel Hargrove to be considered.

Ruff drew back the curtain and stared out at the countryside rushing past. Already deep in shadow, the land took on an unreal aspect as it slid past the window, constantly changing, constantly darkening.

There was a bad job waiting in Colorado. Hard weather and Cody MacCormack. Just now Justice was not even counting on getting there alive.

3

Dinner was at five-thirty. The others were already there when Justice arrived, still wearing his black suit. They waited at their tables to be served or stood at the bar, drinks in hand.

The conversation lapsed briefly as Ruff entered the dining car and then went on, more quietly. Vice-Premier Chapek, his massive elbow resting on the mahogany of the bar, stood beside General Ankirat. The dim light of the wall lamps glistened on Ankirat's bald head, reflected in his monocle.

Captain Saranevo was not there, his being a minor rank in this assemblage, but Zardan was, sitting alone in a shadowed corner, his eyes on Ruff from the moment he entered the room. And so was Colonel Hargrove.

He sat across from the Baroness at the long banquet table, his composure regained, apparently, or his sense of propriety. A senior officer doesn't fly off the handle in the presence of visiting foreign dignitaries no matter the provocation.

Ruff crossed the room, and the Baroness offered her pale, languid hand. Ruff kissed it lightly, smiled and received a smile in return, and seated himself beside the Baroness without being asked.

"Now we can be served," the Baroness said. Ruff glanced at Colonel Hargrove. His face was stone just then, his gray eyes staring at some point a hundred miles distant.

At some unseen signal from the Baroness the party moved over to the banquet table, and minutes later two waiters who moved with the stiffness of military men, which they were, served dinner and poured wine.

Oysters were served, and then asparagus in Hollandaise sauce, followed by an oriental salad with water chestnuts and slivered almonds. Then they were each given a trout bathed in butter, garnished with parsley. Later there were steaks smothered in mushrooms, tender enough to be cut with a fork, black on the outside, pink as salmon on the inside.

After dinner coffee was served, laced with Irish whiskey for those who wanted it, and then the inevitable brandy and cigars.

The waiters cleaned up, and Ruff noticed the big Schofield pistol under the white coat of one of them. Hargrove had made a point of not looking at Justice throughout dinner. Now he rose, with a few murmured polite words to the Baroness, and moved to the bar, where he stood talking with the vice-premier.

The train had slowed somewhat as it rushed on through the night. They would be approaching the coastal mountains, the Diablo Range, Justice knew. Already the air was cooler, and the Baroness, noticing it as well, signaled to Saranevo, who had reappeared, to light the fire in the huge bronze-embellished woodstove at the front of the car.

"You see," the Baroness said with a laugh, "this is roughing it for me. I am afraid I'm quite spoiled. Even a little chill demands instant attention. I'm sure I don't know how my sister can dream of living in the wilderness."

"Well, Lita's got a man to keep her warm," Justice said, leaning across the table. "Maybe that's all she needs."

"It does no harm," Sophia answered quietly. She let her finger run around the rim of her half-empty brandy snifter. "Does it get so terrible up in those mountains, Mr. Justice?"

"Terrible." He leaned back again. "Cold enough to freeze a grizzly to the bone. A horse can't survive—there's no forage. Waterfalls are frozen in their motion. Men, and animals as well, have turned to cannibalism. The winter is a savage thing in the Rockies, ma'am. The winds will cut you in half. Walking those high trails is a descent into frozen hell. There's ice under the snow, you see, buffeting winds, hard weather a man can't see through. And so nothing moves after the snows set in.

"To move is to die, to become lost, to starve. Yet to remain where you are is to freeze slowly. Yes, ma'am, it's terrible when any misstep can break a leg and the nearest doctor is so far off he doesn't seem to be in the same world, when the blood freezes in a man's veins . . . it's terrible. The most terrible place on earth. And," he added with a softness which surprised the Baroness, "the most beautiful."

"You've been there before, then?"

"More than once. It was terrible then; it will be terrible this time."

General Ankirat and Colonel Hargrove had wandered over, and the Baroness invited them to sit.

"Mr. Justice was just telling me about the Rocky Mountain winters. Do you realize what you're heading into, Colonel Hargrove?"

"Yes," the colonel said rigidly. "I've been in the area before, ma'am."

"Oh, have you? You must tell us of your adventures there. Mr. Justice, I'm afraid, is quite reticent when it comes to speaking of himself except with the widest generalities."

"I don't wonder," Hargrove said.

General Ankirat sat, but the colonel remained standing. Zardan had drifted over to stand behind and slightly to his left. The dark man had a razor-thin smile on his lips, and he watched Justice with all the interest of a hawk studying a field mouse.

"Won't you tell us of your western adventures, colonel?" the Baroness urged.

"All right." He nodded stiffly. "If you like. It may be entertaining."

The iron wheels clacked on in an easy cadence beneath the floor. The lamplight shaded the strong features of Colonel Bryson Hargrove. All eyes were on him except those of Ruff Justice, and he began.

"Some years ago I was the commanding officer at Fort Lyon in eastern Colorado. A band of Arapaho renegades had jumped the Indian Agency and taken to the hills under a man called Crazy Jack.

"Crazy Jack," the colonel told them, "as so many of these renegade leaders are, claimed to be inspired by his god to make war. The words of his god were quite vengeful, it seems. He was to let no white live, not a woman, not a child. And Jack followed this commandment with ruthless integrity."

The colonel was silent a minute. He drained his glass and set it back on the table. The train was rounding a bend now, and he braced himself slightly.

"And so, dear Baroness, we went after Jack. Winter was coming in heavily. Three feet of snow overnight the day before we left. The tracking was difficult, the conditions impossible. Yet I had good men with me, and we had closed the gap on Jack, following a bloody trail he left across Colorado.

"Finally we had him cornered, or thought it probable that we did, in a deep canyon not far from Altas Montana. The snowstorm had turned into a blizzard—we couldn't see our horses' heads when we rode, let alone the trail through that wickedly hazardous canyon, so we sent a scout ahead.

"He was a good scout, that man, and I trusted him. He was to return if he saw Jack's camp or indications of an ambush. If he did not find Jack, he was to ride on through to Leadville and wait for us there.

"The scout was a brave man—he had to be to go off on his own through that weather in an area crowded with hostiles of the worst sort. But perhaps his courage failed him on that day. He was a drinking man, a hard-drinking man, and he dredged up more courage from the bottle. Then a little more and a little more.

"We waited, Baroness, but the scout did not return. I gave him an extra day, knowing the conditions ahead. When he did not return after that, we knew the canyon to be clear. Jack had somehow eluded us, and so, with winter settling in, I led my patrol forward into the canyon, wanting to make Leadville ourselves.

"Two miles in, Crazy Jack hit us. They came up out of the storm and they ripped us apart. Two men survived. The rest were slaughtered, staining the blood of Altas Montana Canyon crimson."

"And the scout?" the Baroness asked. "He too was murdered, undoubtedly."

"The scout, who had taken another, safer pass, was already in Leadville, roaring drunk in a saloon . . . the

Lucky Drover, wasn't it, Justice? Or can you remember? How could you? The scout was Ruffin T. Justice, ma'am," the colonel said, and Baroness Mancek noticed that Ruff's fists were clenched, his face tense, the cords in his neck protruding. "A drunken deserter. A coward, a murderer."

The colonel's voice was soft, but it wavered badly. General Ankirat peered at Ruff through his monocle lens. Zardan, against the wall, arms folded, smirked slightly.

"And now you know, Baroness, why Mr. Justice does not drink liquor. Of course it is too late, much too late, for that to make any difference, and I doubt it appeases the demons which must ride with him. Goodnight," the colonel said abruptly. "I have spoken too much, and the old ghosts are beginning to haunt me again."

When the colonel was gone, Ruff sat looking at his hands on the table before him. It was General Ankirat who spoke:

"And have you no rejoinder, Mr. Justice?"

"I don't have to respond to such incredible gossip," Ruff said slowly.

"But usually, when a man makes no show of protest, sir, it indicates—"

"I don't give a damn what you think it indicates, general."

"But this man is now employed by you, Baroness," Vice-Premier Chapek said, his huge bulk blocking out a lantern so that he stood in silhouette before them. "If the colonel's allegations are true, can he be trusted?"

"Are they true, Justice?" the Baroness asked.

"True to the colonel." He stood, his chair nearly tipping over. "I've told you before, why I left the army is not your business. If you want to fire me, stop the train and I'll get off right here. As the colonel has pointed out," he added with a wistful smile, "I do not drink now."

He looked from the vice-premier to the Baroness and then nodded. "I assume that means I am still employed. Goodnight. Dinner was excellent."

He turned then and walked toward the door, and all their eyes followed him. Ruff stepped between cars, the blast of wind which met him cold and stiff. Entering the second car, he found it empty, as it should have been. Only Colonel Hargrove had retired, and his compartment was on the other side of the small parlor, in the rear half of the Pullman.

Ruff opened his compartment and stepped in. He stopped abruptly, his hand reaching for his shoulder holster. Something was wrong, but it was a moment before he discovered what it was.

His eyes gradually adjusted to the darkness, and the slumped figure on the floor was defined against the blackness. Without turning on the lamp, Ruff bent to examine the man.

It was Captain Saranevo, and he was quite dead, his neck twisted back, snapped cleanly. Ruff locked his compartment door and crossed to the window. With some effort he raised the window, the cold gusting air sweeping into the compartment with the rush of sounds the clacking train made as it climbed the mountain grade.

They were approaching a trestle now. The moon was rising above the mountain peaks, and it silvered the land. A deep, precipitous gorge lay beneath the trestle, and white water painted a thin pale line far below against the bluish-black of the rocks.

Ruff waited until the train had rolled onto the trestle, waited a second longer until they were nearly at midpoint, above the river far below, and then he hefted

Saranevo, shoving his head and shoulders through the window.

With a heave he lifted Saranevo's limp legs and shoved hard. The captain tumbled from the train, bounced once on the trestle's edge, and then cartwheeled slowly through space, falling silently toward the dim river far, far below.

Ruff closed the window and only then lit the lantern. There was no blood, no sign of disturbance other than a rumpled bed cover.

He undressed, turned the lamp down again, and slid into bed, his Colt .41 beneath his pillow. Why Saranevo, and why here and now?

He knew someone had been poking in his things. Perhaps Saranevo had returned to do a little more sleuthing. Perhaps in the darkness someone had taken him for Ruff Justice. Whoever it was had tremendous strength. The captain's neck had been snapped like a twig. Ruff thought instantly of the Colter brothers. Hurly and Clive both were built like grizzlies. They had a grudge against Ruff, of course, and it wouldn't be that difficult to walk forward into this car from their own with everyone at dinner.

It could also be that Saranevo was killed elsewhere—for unknown reasons—and dumped in Ruff's compartment to throw suspicion on him. That, along with Colonel Hargrove's story, might be enough to cause the Baroness to give in to the general's urging and have the train halted and Ruff Justice put off.

Whatever the reason, there was a killer on board. And of all the people on board this train winding through the mountains, he could count none of them as friends. He would sleep lightly, and that Colt would never be far from his hand.

Yawning, Ruff rolled over, curling up into the blanket. There was no use in thinking about the Saranevo business any longer; there was not enough to solve it with. As for sitting awake the night long, gun in hand, or raising the alarm, he had no intention of doing either. A man needs sleep most desperately in times of trouble. He had seen death before, violent death. He had never liked it, but he was damned if it was going to rob him of sleep. As for raising the alarm, he would only be pointing his finger at himself by doing so.

He yawned again and forced his mind to empty, to go dark and fuzzy, and after a minute's lingering tension, he fell into a gentle sleep.

The train had slowed almost to a standstill, and when it began to pick up on the downgrade after cresting the Diablos and make its mad rush into the great California Valley beyond, the cars cracked like a whip twice.

Ruff thought at first that this was what had awakened him. He peered out of his window, seeing the heavily shadowed valley floor far below, the distant looming bulk of the towering Sierra Nevada.

Crossing the room on bare feet, Ruff listened, his ear against the door. Slowly he opened it, only a crack, and he saw the small figure hurrying away down the dark corridor.

The cook with the huge mustache, the one called Benny. And what was he doing there?

Ruff closed the door. It was probably nothing. Maybe the man had only now finished with his cleaning up and was making his way back to the sleeping car. Maybe.

Ruff sat on the edge of the bed. The room was chill against his naked body. He had begun to slip into bed when he again heard the whisper of footsteps in the corridor. He rose instantly and, panther-silent, moved beside his door, the gun in his hand.

The tapping was very soft; at first he was not sure it was at his door. Slowly his hand reached out, gripping the cold brass of the knob.

When he opened it he moved quickly, coming to face the open doorway with his Colt leveled.

She stood there in gossamer, her raven-black hair brushed down across her shoulders. The thin light bled through the flimsy white nightgown and outlined her magnificent body.

"You won't need that," the Baroness said, nodding toward his gun. Her eyes swept over his naked body, and for a minute Ruff did not move as a slow smile turned up the corners of her full mouth. "I would like to come in eventually," the Baroness Sophia said, and Ruff backed into the darkened room. She followed him, silently closing the door, silently latching it.

"What is it . . . ?" Ruff began, but she pressed against him and her full, parted lips sought his, and the question became meaningless and died in his throat as his body responded to hers.

His hand followed the knuckles of her spine to the small of her back and then down along the swell of her buttocks, which were firm, silky beneath the fabric of her sheer gown.

"Did I disturb you?" the Baroness murmured, her lips tugging at his ear lobe, her breath soft and moist against his flesh.

"You are," Ruff said. He kissed the nape of her neck and let his mouth slide along the smooth scented flesh until he could taste the soft upswelling of her breasts, the scent of jasmine tingling in his nostrils. Her heart pulsed beneath his lips as he kissed her.

"I didn't want to bother you," she said breathlessly. Her fingers were in his hair. She sagged against him as if her bones had turned to liquid beneath that nearly transparent, flawless skin.

"It's always nice to make new friends," Ruff said. He lifted his head and smiled at her. His fingers untied the two bows which fastened the bodice of her nightgown.

"You said you never mixed business and bed," she reminded him.

"I promise not to think of business once."

Her nightdress fell open and her firm, full breasts peered shyly out. Ruff made them welcome with lingering kisses, his lips lingering on the taut pink nipples. His hands rested on her thighs, pressing her near to him.

Slowly he led her back to his bed. She stepped from the nightgown she wore, letting it rustle to the floor, and she stood there illuminated by the silver moonlight which fell through a part in the drapes. White as ivory, as poised and graceful as a sculptor's marble. His eyes swept over her with amazement and hunger, following the flow of her breasts, which rose and fell now with excitement, the tapered line of her thighs, which ended in a mysterious patch of soft, coal-black down.

She came to him, smiling as she studied Ruff's naked form reclining on the bed. She got to her knees beside him, and her hands, her lips roamed his lean body.

Sophia kissed his inner thighs, let her lips burrow between them as her hand drifted across his hard abdomen. Her kisses led her to his knees, his calves. She administered two soft kisses to the bridge of his feet and then worked her way slowly back up as her hands lightly brushed across his crotch. She gasped, almost as in amazement.

Her breath was warm against his thighs, warm against his abdomen, and she turned slowly, slipping into his bed, her flesh smooth against his. He felt the soft touch of her thighs against his, felt a brief, tantalizing warm moistness against his leg as she straddled him.

He put his hands on her knees, let them travel up across her fluid hips and along her waist to her breasts, cupping them in his palms.

Sophia threw her dark, extremely long hair back across her white shoulders, and he could see the smile on her lips by the moonlight. Her teeth glinted white; her eyes were nearly shut, and she moved against him infinitesimally, her pelvis barely in contact with his, her movements self-absorbed, maddening.

Her hands dipped between his legs, and she measured him, hefted him, sent a chill of anticipation crawling up her own spine. He was warm, his blood pulsing strongly, and slowly Sophia lifted herself and positioned Ruff.

She settled on him with a shudder. Her head fell forward suddenly as if she could not hold it up, and he felt the trembling of her thighs as she melted against him, taking him in slow increments.

At last it was done, and she locked herself around him, the tiny muscles within her rippling with overexcitement. She felt a gradual loosening, a seeping of warmth, and she began to sway against him, her hair, which fell now across her beautiful face, brushing Ruff's chest and abdomen with each motion.

She had begun so slowly, but now she felt a series of electric impulses sweeping through her, sending tingling joy up along her thighs, to her breasts and up her spine to her brain, which could not categorize the impulses as heat or cold, pain or pleasure, but which demanded more and more.

Now her white, very physical hips began to move with intensity, with purpose, and she grasped at him, stroking and then impaling herself on Ruff as her hips twisted and writhed with the grace of an athlete in motion, with the feline grace and passion of a woman.

She fell against Ruff, her breasts flattened against his chest, and her mouth sought his throat, his shoulders, his lips as she sucked at him, bit at his flesh as her hips continued their incessant drive.

Now Ruff had captured her style, her timing, and he began to sway in a counterrhythm, the woman breathing raggedly in his ear, urging him on with words he could not understand, with gasps he could, and the fire which he had sparked in Sophia now threatened to consume him, and he let it.

Their bodies swayed and struggled against one another, demanding a satisfaction which came with a sudden rush, a release, an exhausting, nearly debilitating consummation.

Ruff lay back, stroking her long dark hair, and she continued to murmur, to speak in a strange tongue which he understood fully, to stroke and to probe at his flesh.

She sat up once, and her eyes glittered in the night. Her face glowed and seemed distant, angelic. It was slack and nearly reverent. Impulse tugged Ruff's interest, and he drew her tightly to him, beginning the slow steady swaying until she panted: "Let me rest. I need to rest awhile. God, you are a man!"

She sagged against him, her heart pounding, and Ruff let his head rest against the pillow. He closed his eyes for a minute, lulled by her soft touches, her gentle, disjointed words.

The door clicked open, and Ruff pawed at his eyes, sitting up, reaching automatically for his gun. But it was only Sophia. She had gone. Somehow he had fallen off to sleep and she had slipped from his bed. He caught only a momentary glimpse of her white calf before the door clicked shut.

He sat on the edge of the bed for a moment, head hanging, a smile on his lips. Then he rose and locked the door again.

The train lurched on through the night, but it no longer seemed like a friendless train, and the journey would now not seem so long. He lay in his bed where the soft, mingled scents of Sophia still lingered, and he closed his eyes, drifting off to an easy, deep sleep.

It was long past midnight when he awoke again. The

sheets were cold and the floor, rumbling beneath his feet, was like ice.

Yet it was time. He glanced at his watch by moonlight and dressed swiftly, silently. He slid his boots on and slipped into his shoulder holster. It was time to have a little look around the Baroness's train.

4

THE CORRIDOR WAS dark when Ruff stepped out of his compartment, quietly closing the door behind him. There was a ribbon of light under the door to the room next to his, and as he watched it was extinguished. The Baroness's compartment.

He moved swiftly to the parlor room, which was empty, and crossing it, he opened the door to the rear of the car, which contained more sleeping quarters. Ruff slipped through that corridor and slipped out into the night, a gust of cold wind reaching out to slap at him.

The next car was the sleeping car for Mix and his crew, the servants, and the enlisted personnel. Through the smoked glass of the doorway window Ruff saw a blur of shadow approaching him, and he stepped back into the Pullman behind him, turning off the hall lamp which hung above the door.

The train rolled beneath him, and as he watched, an armed man, too indistinct to identify, stepped out onto the platform between the two cars and stood smoking a cigar.

He had a rifle slung over his shoulder and wore a bulky coat, the collar turned up to make identification impossible in this light.

The man turned his back to Ruff, and then he saw the brief spray of sparks as the man threw his cigar away. After a minute, the guard, who was hopping up and down trying to keep warm, turned and went back into the car.

Ruff eased out of the Pullman and went to the window, peering in. The men slept in rows of bunks along the wall. There was an iron stove with a pipe running at an angle to the ceiling and little else. The commoners were roughing it.

Ruff glanced up and then quickly back toward the Pullman. The iron ladder was to his left, and Ruff swung out, grasping it.

In moments he was on the roof of the swaying car, the wind stiff in his face, tugging at his clothes. Soot and cinders swirled up and stung his eyes. He heard the door bang shut beneath him, and he crouched low.

Going to his belly, Ruff leaned over the edge and saw the guard, tin coffee cup in hand. Ruff eased back from the edge of the car and made his way along the catwalk. Once he tripped over a ventilator and came down hard on a knee.

Cursing silently, he put an ear to the roof, but he heard nothing, so perhaps no one had heard him. Moving more cautiously in the nearly total darkness, he reached the end of the car and peered over.

He drew his head back immediately. There was another guard in front of the baggage car. He lay pressed against the shifting roof of the car, noticing the faint yellow light from the caboose. The moon shifted behind the clouds to the west, and Ruff lay utterly still. He was illuminated as if by a beacon, and the guard had turned toward him, his eyes going skyward.

Then Ruff saw him stiffen and reach for the rifle which was slung across his shoulder.

There was no time for long decisions. Ruff got to his feet and lunged with a single motion. He slammed into the guard just as the man got his rifle to his shoulder, and they collided roughly with the door behind him.

Ruff stood dizzily and got an arm up just in time to fend off a desperate blow thrown by the guard. The man's fist bounced painfully off Ruff's forearm, and Ruff drove his head into the guard's belly, knocking him back against the door of the freight car. The breath whooshed from the guard, but he was a game one.

He lashed out with a left and then tried to knee Justice. But Ruff had expected that, and he crossed a knee over, deflecting the blow. Then, feinting left, Ruff threw a hard right which connected solidly with the guard's neck just below the jawline, and the man staggered back, blinking his eyes.

From his belt the guard produced a handgun, and Ruff saw it nearly too late in the bad light. The pistol stabbed flame, and Ruff jerked his head to one side. He kicked out savagely, catching the guard high in the chest, and the man rocked back against the rail, his feet coming up from the platform.

For a moment he balanced there, wide-eyed, and then without a sound he tumbled over. Ruff tried the door on the baggage car. His breath was coming in ragged gasps. The door was locked solidly, and now with alarm he realized that a light had gone on in the barracks car. He heard rapid muttering, and the sound of approaching boots.

He would not have believed the guard's shot could be heard above the clank and rumble of the train, but apparently it had been. Perhaps someone had just happened to glance out the window and had seen the struggling shadows—no matter, they were coming.

In a split second Ruff was to the ladder and clambering for the roof. The door burst open behind him, and there was a confusion of words.

He ran along the catwalk, head down. Once he nearly misstepped, but caught his balance and rushed on. He cursed again. The hall light in the Pullman was on once more, indicating that someone was patrolling there.

He eased to the edge of the car, saw the bulky guard still sipping his coffee, and instantly realized he was trapped if anyone had a look-see from the other ladder.

His heart thumped in his ribcage, his stomach knotted. He was nearly ready to take his chances with the guard when he saw the guard turn and open the door to the barracks car, calling something.

Ruff didn't hesitate. The moment the guard's head was turned he launched himself toward the roof of the Pullman.

He landed hard, skinning an elbow, slamming the breath from himself, and for a few seconds he could not find a grip and he slid slowly toward the edge of the car. Scrambling to the catwalk, he dragged himself to the edge of the roof.

Looking over, he saw the guard, apparently undisturbed by events. Yet his rifle was in his hands now. From time to time he glanced anxiously toward the barracks car.

Ruff slipped away from the edge and went forward, carefully making his way to the front of the Pullman. He was very nearly over his own quarters, but there was no way down. Someone was up and active in the car. Perhaps they had already checked his compartment, though he doubted it.

Cautiously he leaned over the front of the sleeping car

and noticed the lights on in this end as well. He decided to brazen it out.

Ruff clambered down, dropping noiselessly to the platform. He crossed to the dining car in front of him, first checking to make sure it was empty. He walked the length of the darkened dining car and went to the bar.

He pulled down a bottle of Irish whiskey, took a deep drink, and splashed some on his shirt. He looked at the ruffles of that shirt and saw that they were black with soot. He tore the cuffs off and jammed them into his pocket. Wiping his face and dusting his suit with a napkin, he strolled back toward the Pullman.

As he opened the door, Zardan stepped out to confront him. There was a smile on the dark man's lips, but it was not a particularly nice expression. Zardan had his hand thrust casually into his coat pocket, and Ruff would have bet the moon that he had a casual little pistol wrapped in his fingers.

"You are up late, Mr. Justice," Zardan said smoothly.

"I sometimes have trouble sleeping."

"Oh?" He nodded. "I can understand that."

He had caught the scent of whiskey, and now his smile broadened a little. "Is that bay rum I detect?"

"Look, Zardan," Ruff said confidentially. "I need this job." He moved closer to the smaller man. "I don't drink much, but sometimes . . . well, when you need it."

"It will be our little secret," Zardan said.

Ruff thanked him and then excused himself, stepping around Zardan as he went to his compartment. He stepped inside and locked the door, taking a deep breath. He lit the lantern briefly and examined his face. It was smudged at the temples and on the point of the chin, but perhaps he had gotten away with it in the dim light of the corridor.

Ruff lay down on his bunk, fully dressed, reeking of

whiskey, and he watched the door for long minutes before he again fell off to sleep.

Daylight was a fierce crimson globe beaming against the window of Ruff's compartment. There was the shrill grating of iron against iron and the sounds of steam being gradually released. Ruff went to the window, parted the curtains, and saw they were slowing near a small ramshackle town, probably for water and fuel.

He washed his face, dug his ebony-handled razor from his case, and lathered his shaving soap. That done, he splashed on some bay rum, recalling Zardan's remarks.

The man was no fool, but he just might have found Ruff's excuse convincing enough. Frowning as he examined his dark suit in daylight, Ruff took out his buckskins and dressed, exchanging his dark hat for the white one with beadwork on the band.

He picked up his torn shirt, remembering the cuffs in his coat pocket, and jammed it into the trash container in the corner.

Then, brushing his hair back across his shoulders, combing his mustache with his fingers, he planted his hat and stepped to the suitcase on his bunk, removing his gunbelt.

He strapped the long-barreled .44 on, positioned his Bowie behind him, and out of long habit checked the loads in his pistol.

He was glad he had. The pistol was fully loaded, but something he could not put his finger on caused him to remove the cartridges from the cylinder and examine them.

He saw instantly that the bullets had been scored, probably by a pair of pliers. Shallow, bright scoring appeared against the dark lead. Prying the bullets apart himself, Ruff frowned with surprise.

He dumped the powder into his hand, only it was not powder at all. He sniffed it, and the strong acrid scent of sodium nitrate filled his nostrils. He tapped out the cartridge and tried another. All of them had been tampered with, all filled with enough nitroglycerine to blow a man's head off.

Ruff dumped the cartridges into the trash and then emptied his gunbelt after a cursory examination showed that he had been well provided with those little caps of dynamite. It was nice to have friends.

It was a clever idea and one Ruff had never heard of before. It could never be proved. The primer would detonate the nitro and split the barrel of that Colt like a tin can.

It would be a shame—a defective weapon. And Ruff Justice would be six feet under.

He dug out the new boxes of .44s he had purchased at the '49er Outfitters and bit the lead off of one. He tipped the cartridge, got a reassuring handful of black-powder grains, and reloaded his pistol.

Ruff stepped off the train and onto the platform of the forlorn little whistlestop. The sign on the station, faded and peeling, read "Grand Junction." The town sat in the middle of a wide, undeveloped valley where the grass was yellow with drought and dust hung heavily in the air.

Beside the station there was a combination hotel and dry-goods store. Set back a ways from the tracks was a saloon, which could be reached through a vacant lot overgrown with weeds and littered with broken bottles and tin cans.

From the barracks car men appeared and streamed toward it. Those in second class hadn't had the amenities of the Baroness's party, and they were thirsty.

Ruff stood in the dry shade of the platform and studied the departing soldiers. Eventually Mix appeared, followed by Clive and Hurly. Hurly, his arm strapped tightly to his side, had to be helped down from the train, and he grimaced with pain.

Clive touched Gorman Mix on the shoulder and said something, and Ruff saw the badman's head come around. They stood together looking at the tall man in buckskins and then trudged off toward the saloon.

Three red-coated soldiers stood along the train at intervals, and Ruff knew as many were stationed on the other side. He stood on the platform, leaning against an upright, thumbs hooked into his belt.

He thought for a moment of Sophia, warm and tender in the night, and then of the man who liked to cut open sticks of dynamite and dump the powder into other men's cartridges. No one seemed excited about the missing guard, he observed, nor had anyone yet mentioned that Captain Saranevo was missing—perhaps no one but Ruff and the killer knew as yet.

As he watched, the Baroness came onto the platform of her Pullman and detrained with a flourish. The baggage handler, dozing in the sun at the far end of the platform, came suddenly alert as Sophia, in a deep-blue gown, stepped down with the assistance of General Ankirat, his medals glittering in the sunlight.

The Baroness glanced toward Ruff but looked as quickly away. Vice-Premier Chapek appeared, blinking into the brilliant sunlight, and then Colonel Hargrove, looking pale and severe. Zardan stayed on the train.

The Baroness swept grandly into the depot, the general at her heels, and Ruff wandered that way. When he reached the heavy depot door he saw the Baroness and her party in an alcove to one side. He saw the station manager bowing and fluttering around her, and he smiled.

Colonel Hargrove detached himself from the group. Ruff heard him mutter something about "army business," and he watched with cool eyes as the American officer crossed the empty station to the telegraph window.

He scribbled something out and pushed it into the telegrapher's window, paid with two silver dollars, and then rejoined the Baroness's party.

Ruff went back outside into the dry, cool morning and circled the station. With deliberate motions he collected a half-dozen bottles and as many cans from the littered field.

He walked to the disused corral behind the depot and positioned them. Inside the depot, the first shot rang loudly, and Hargrove turned sharply toward the back door, his hand dropping to the butt of his own revolver. Sophia looked from the door to the general, who had stiffened. Slowly they followed Colonel Hargrove. The porch of the saloon filled with curious men. Gorman Mix was holding a bottle by the neck, leaning across the rail. Zardan watched with a faint smile from the platform of the Pullman.

Ruffin Justice lifted his pistol and fired again. The bottle, at twenty paces, exploded, as did the one next to it as he fired again. Another shot sent a can whining off the corral rail.

Ruff lowered his Colt and opened the loading gate. He thumbed in fresh cartridges from his belt and only then seemed aware of the crowd he had drawn. His eyebrows lifted in mock astonishment.

"What's the matter?"

"You frightened us," the Baroness said. She toyed with her gold necklace; her dark eyes were wide.

"I did? Only a little target practice, Baroness. Something to pass the time."

Then he holstered his Colt and without looking at any of them or the men who lingered on the porch of the saloon, Ruff Justice walked leisurely back toward the waiting train.

No one had been into his compartment this time. He knew because he had taken the time to throw a ball of paper on the floor before squeezing out. It was still where he had left it. To an intruder it would only appear that Mr. Justice was a little messy with his trash, and he had found it an effective, simple alarm in times past.

In another fifteen minutes, refueled and watered, they were on their way once more, rumbling out of the long valley toward the distantly looming, snow-peaked Sierra Nevada.

Lunch was a silent affair. The Baroness complained of the heat, which had smothered the valley floor as the sun rose higher, and of the motion, which she said disturbed her appetite.

Vice-Premier Chapek drank his lunch as he drank most of his meals. A mountain of a man, the quarts of liquor seemed to have no effect on him. His glittering little eyes were always sharp, penetrating.

Someone mentioned that a guard, apparently drunk, had fallen overboard during the night, and Ruff glanced up to see Zardan's eyes directly on him. Ruff stared blandly at him, finished his ham, and dabbed at his mustache, offering no comment.

The colonel was absent, and that bothered Ruff. Protocol demanded attentiveness to visiting dignitaries of the Baroness's rank; but perhaps Hargrove also had an upset stomach—with Ruff at the root of it.

They rolled on. Once after noon Ruff decided to see how far brass would get him, and he strolled through the train to the barracks car. The massive guard on duty nodded amiably but put a hand on Ruff's wrist when he tried to open the door.

"Just wanted to talk to the other Americans, my friends," Ruff said with a smile. "Mix, and the big men."

"No." The guard had little English, but he had that

word down pat. He repeated it twice more, his viselike grip steady on Ruff's wrist, and Justice shrugged, turning away.

He napped in his room until dark, then joined the others for the evening meal. Colonel Hargrove was there, his eyes flinty, but Zardan was nowhere to be seen. They ate in virtual silence, with the Baroness sparing an occasional melting glance for Ruff.

Back in his compartment, Ruff propped himself up on his bunk, waiting for the hours to pass. Once he heard someone in the hall and peeked out expectantly, but it was not the Baroness, who really did seem to be feeling ill.

He recognized the shadowy figure instantly, but it puzzled him. The cook, Benny, was listening at the general's door. At the creak of the hinges of Ruff's door the man bent down and picked up a piece of cutlery which was at his feet. He turned, smiling beneath that huge mustache, and walked away. It was a clumsy job, and Ruff wasn't taken in for a minute.

He closed the door again and spent an aimless hour staring out the window. The mountains were nearer, cutting jagged silhouettes against the sky. The moon blued the white-capped peaks and deepened the shadows. The train rushed on, beginning its ascent up along snake-sided canyons and over wild mountain streams. The window against his cheek was cold. The train was rushing toward winter, and a hard winter it would be here and in the still-distant Rockies.

Ruff rose and shook himself, clearing away the cobwebs of lethargy. He glanced at his watch, which rested open on the bureau, and strapped on his gun. It was time to pay a little visit to Colonel Bryson Hargrove.

5

RUFF EASED DOWN the corridor and through the parlor room. He tapped on the second door, his hand resting on the worn walnut butt of his Colt. When Colonel Hargrove opened the door, Ruff slipped in.

The colonel was in pajamas and an army blue robe. As Ruff sat on the colonel's bed, Hargrove stuffed a blanket in the crack beneath the door. Then he lit the lantern and turned with a grin.

"You damnable rascal, you," he said, sticking out his hand. They shook hands warmly and smiled at each other for the first time.

"How are you, colonel?"

"Fine, Ruff. Just fine. And you—despite the heavy drinking?" He peered at Justice.

"Doesn't affect some of us so much as others," Ruff replied with a smile. "But you did lay it on a little. I thought maybe you'd add a clincher and take a poke at me for a while."

"If I'd thought of it . . . by God!" Hargrove rubbed his chin thoughtfully. "But it worked. I've even heard rumors that you're up and about sneaking liquor."

"Zardan bought that, then?"

"With him, who knows? He's sharp and very tricky. But are you having any luck, Ruff?"

"Not so's you'd notice, sir. Damned if I can penetrate to the baggage car. But I'll have another try."

"We'll get in. Fortunately we've a man on our side, a good man. Captain Saranevo is . . ."

"Captain Saranevo is dead," Ruff told him. The colonel's face stiffened.

"How? When?"

Ruff told him about it briefly. "I had to dump him out my window. It's funny no one's mentioned that, isn't it?"

"Damned funny. Unless they're on to us." Colonel Hargrove sat on his bunk next to Ruff. The officer's eyes were bleared, heavily pouched. "You're right in between, aren't you, Justice? Half of the people on this train need you in Colorado. Need you badly. The other half would stop at nothing to keep you from getting there alive."

"That's about where it stands," Ruff admitted with a smile. "The Baroness—"

His voice broke off abruptly. He stood and eased to the door, putting his finger to his lips. Muffled footsteps drifted away down the carpeted corridor. There was nothing else, so after a moment Ruff returned to the bunk.

"The Baroness definitely wants me to arrive. I'm not sure any of the others give a damn one way or the other. Mix wants me dead, certainly. Someone has already given it a try." He told Hargrove about the doctored cartridges.

"Just dumped dynamite into your shells, did they?

Damned clever. So that's what the target practice was all about—that one had me wondering."

"That's it," Ruff said. "Someone got the message."

"Mix?"

"Seems too clever for him, colonel. Besides, it's no easier for him to get through the train than for me."

"Likely it was done before you got on board."

"I don't know. I'll be glad to get off this train, though. I need a little room to maneuver, sir."

"Don't we all. Dammit to hell," he said, suddenly exasperated. "All this diplomatic privilege has our hands neatly tied, doesn't it, Ruff? We're teetering on the brink of an international incident right now. I wonder," he mused, "how I'd look in a buck private's uniform."

"Just keep your head low, sir. Let me take the risks."

"You'll have to, but I don't like it. If those asses in Washington could forget about the damned 'book' for once . . . but they won't." He sighed.

"They would if they knew Stone Eyes as we do, wouldn't they, sir?"

"That they would, Ruff, that they would. But the reality of this is that we're out on a limb by ourselves and the bad guys have the pruning saw." He stood, his face drawn, his eyes serious, sadder than Ruff could remember seeing them. "You just keep your own head low, boy." He rested a hand on Ruff's shoulder and said with a smile, "And lay off the booze."

"I'll do my best," Ruff answered. The colonel turned the lamp down, and they removed the blanket from the crack beneath the door. Ruff listened for a minute, letting his eyes grow accustomed to the darkness, then, opening the door only a hair, he looked down the corridor. He turned then and nodded to Colonel Hargrove, then slipped out to merge with the shadows of the corridor.

Ruff had a thought, and he strode to the end of the

corridor, past Chapek's room. Reaching up, he pulled the chimney from the lantern and stripped the wick. At least for tonight that corridor would be dark.

He made his way back through the empty parlor compartment to his own end of the corridor. The lantern at that end was extinguished too, and Ruff made sure it would stay that way, yanking the wick from it as well.

He turned then toward his own compartment. He was just passing the door to the Baroness's room, and he ground his teeth in silent agitation when it opened suddenly.

She stood there bathed in diffused light, wearing a white silk wrapper. Her hair was knotted loosely at the base of her neck.

"I thought I heard someone," she said.

"Just me. I thought I'd like to talk to you." Ruff leaned casually against the door jamb, crossing his arms. Sophia smiled, but she shook her head.

"I'm really not feeling well. This travel . . ."

"It's all right," Ruff said, concealing the relief he felt. He reached out and touched her dark, silky hair, and she smiled wanly.

"It's just that I really don't feel well."

"You don't have to apologize," he said. In truth she didn't look that well, but the way she gripped the door made Ruff wonder if someone else wasn't in that room. At any rate he had blundered onto an excuse for being in the corridor at this hour.

Anyone listening would have caught the familiarity in the Baroness's voice and realized that Ruff was trying to play man-games in the night. Of course, he realized bleakly, that might be enough to give someone else the idea of killing him.

They said goodnight, Ruff lingering as if he could not tear himself away. Then he returned again to his own compartment.

He drew back his curtain and with plummeting confidence saw that it had begun to snow across the Sierras. Wet flakes clung to the bluish pane of glass and slid away. Beyond, the dark ranks of pines in the gorges were smothered with snow. Up higher it was coming down hard, and they were still climbing, driving toward it.

From the packet of goods he had purchased in San Francisco, Ruff took a coil of hemp rope. Hardly trusting now, he examined it for cuts. Finding none, he looped the rope over his shoulder and opened his window.

The wind that drove through the opening was edged with icy steel. It was nearly enough to drive him back on his heels. It was much worse out there than he had thought. Snow flitted into the room, rimed the floor, and melted, being replaced by fresh snow.

Ruff crossed to his door and stuck a cautious head out. Zardan had the habit of popping up unexpectedly, and now that he thought of it, so did the cook. But no one was about in the darkened corridor of the Pullman. Ruff pulled the door to and turned swiftly toward the front of the car and out into the freezing cold.

The wind mauled his back and shoulders as he climbed the icy rungs of the iron ladder to the roof of the Pullman.

On the catwalk he came erect, and the wind drove him off balance. He got to his hands and knees, finding a thin coating of ice on the roof, fresh snow over that.

He paced off six steps and tied the rope to the catwalk over where he judged his open window to be. He tugged the knot, checking the rope again, then, keeping low against the thrust of the wind, he worked his way toward the rear of the train.

It was almost too late when he saw it. Ruff flattened out instantly and it whipped past. A snow-heavy pine bough from an overhanging tree had nearly taken him off his feet. Well, it would be a neat way to go, he thought grimly, simply swept away and crushed by the iron wheels. No sign of Mr. Justice.

It happened once more before he reached the tail end of the Pullman, but Justice was alert for it now and he ducked neatly under the pine bough. The wind was a howling wash of snow now, the ice treacherous underfoot. The train was making a long, gradual turn, and Ruff glanced up through the snow and smoke which ran along the spine of the train. There was a tunnel up ahead somewhere, he knew, a ten-mile tunnel, and he had no wish to be on top when they entered it.

Cautiously he positioned himself on the edge of the Pullman's roof. Leaping from car to car was hazardous—with ice and snow and on a curve, it was damn near suicidal.

Ruff crouched, waited for the wind to subside momentarily, and dove forward. The wind batted at him and knocked him sideways, and for a brief, blood-draining moment he thought he had misjudged it.

But the roof of the trailing Pullman came out to meet him. He crashed against it and was rolled up onto the roof of the second car, the wind twisting him sideways, sucking the breath from his lungs.

Ruff felt himself slipping away, the sheet of ice underneath mocking his attempts to find purchase. His fingertips grooved the thin layer of snow and simply grated over the ice, and he felt his boots go over the side and into space.

There was a ventilator nearby, but he could not reach it. There was nothing but the ice and the snowstorm around him.

He was sliding and could not help himself, slipping slowly, inexorably over. What instinct prompted him he could not have said, but he suddenly found his Bowie in his hand and drove it down with a panicked fury, burying it in the roof of the barracks car.

Panting, he wriggled upward, wrenched the knife free, and repeated the action, reaching far out to drive the point of the bowie into the roof. Gradually he scraped his way to the catwalk, and he sat there for a moment, hunched against the wind, his lungs filled with fire and ice, his hands numb.

He thrust his hands inside his shirt and let them warm. He touched a rib with his icy fingers, and a reflexive gasp of pain convinced him that he had cracked a rib during his leap.

"You're getting too old for this, Mr. Justice," Ruff muttered to himself.

The wind tore at his long hair and drifted it over his face. The fringes on his elkskin shirt flapped and danced madly.

He realized suddenly that he had been sitting there much too long. The cold was working on him already. His thoughts were slightly fuzzed at the edges.

He looked toward the front of the train, but could not see far enough to know if they were approaching the long tunnel. All he got for his trouble was a cinder in the eye. A cinder which had remarkably held its heat through the snowstorm long enough to sting badly.

The train bucked and pitched beneath him now. The wind was coming directly from the flank as the train wound along a treacherous curve. Through a brief gap in the clouds, Ruff saw a plunging, snow-swept canyon beneath them.

He got stiffly to a crouch and walked along the train's roof to the rear of the barracks car. There was no guard.

Of course a man would have to be crazy to stand on that platform on a night like this; but soldiers and gunmen were paid to be a little crazy.

The green, shifting bulk of the freight car was stark

against the white backdrop. Ruff again carefully
searched the platform below him and on the front of the
baggage car. Nothing.

Nothing at all showed through the swirl and toss of
the night but a flat, narrow beam of light from the caboose.

He swung down, clutching the ladder, and crossed to
the baggage car. The door was locked, and Ruff took his
Bowie to it.

A useful implement, that long-bladed knife, he decided. He cut away the wood around the latch, removing it in thick, curling chips. When he had the latch
exposed he slid the bar back with the point of the Bowie
and with a last glance around was into the musty baggage car, out of the thunder of the night storm.

He worked his way by feel along the wall of the baggage car, finding four oversized crates, a large ship's
trunk, a mail sack. Two drums of coal oil sat against the
end wall, secured with a length of chain.

He waited as his eyes adjusted to the darkness. There
was a lantern fixed to the wall above the door, but he
didn't want to risk lighting it, even in this weather, at
this time of night.

It could be the guard who was supposed to be stationed outside was standing his watch in the warmth of
the barracks car. From time to time, if that were the
case, he would be bound to at least peer out at the
baggage car.

Objects appeared indistinctly, drawing out of the
darkness as his eyes slowly adjusted. The sharp lines of
the trunks and crates drew Ruff's attention. The trunk
was locked, but responded to the attentions of the
Bowie. He popped the latch and dug through it, finding
nothing but women's clothing—the Baroness's fancies.

The crates were large enough. New pine, unpainted,
unstenciled. He pried away a slat, which creaked on the

nails, a disturbingly loud sound in the empty baggage car.

Pulling away some packing, Ruff dug inside the crate. His hand found iron. Cold, smooth iron, and his fingers ran along the metal, finally defining the familiar shape of a black iron stove.

The second crate contained an identical stove, and Ruff was beginning to lose his confidence. Somewhere in that baggage car there had to be a key to all of this. But where?

He rose and walked to the walls, gradually working his way along them. And then it came to him—through the nostrils.

He leaned close to the wall and sniffed the fresh paint of the siding. The walls had been newly painted but only along this one wall. There could be many, reasons for that, but Ruff was convinced that there was only one.

He slid his Bowie between a crack in two of the fresh boards and pried. The paneling came away stubbornly. When he had room for his fingers he slid his knife into the sheath at the back of his belt and gripped the board with his hand.

Bracing himself, he pulled, nearly losing his balance and the plank came free in his hands.

Setting it aside, Ruff reached inside the false wall and found what he was looking for. He withdrew his hand. The spanking new Winchester was cool in his grip. He reached in again and withdrew another rifle. Crouching, he searched along the floor of the compartment and found an ammunition box.

The shadow flitted into his vision, and Ruff managed to turn and jam the rifle barrel upward, catching the man on the cheek.

He bellowed, collided with Ruff, and they fell together. Ruff twisted and brought a knee up, but a sledgehammer-like fist fell against his temple, setting off the bells.

He squirmed free, jamming the flat of his hand against the man's nose, and came to his feet. The guard kicked out, taking Ruff on the shin just below the knee. Ruff instantly lost the feeling in that leg. He staggered back, toppling over a crate.

The guard had a club in his hand, and he came out of the darkness, his arm arcing downward. Ruff rolled aside, and the crate behind him splintered as the guard slammed his club against it.

He swung again, and Ruff rolled away, snatching at his Bowie. He came up in a crouch, the knife glinting in his hand, and the guard hesitated, his hand sliding along the wall.

Suddenly he lunged, and something hard and bright flashed before Ruff's eyes. The man had a fire ax, and he wielded it insanely, flailing about, splintering crates, smashing breakables in the dark interior of the baggage car.

Ruff fell back, tipped over the heavy crate containing an iron stove, and felt the wall at his back. The guard leaped to the top of the crate and hefted his ax with two hands.

The blade flashed downward, and Ruff leaped aside, feeling the cold breath of the passing blade beside his ear. Angrily he kicked out, booting the crate from beneath the guard's feet, and the man hit the floor, chin first.

Ruff stood panting over him. He stepped on the guard's wrist and removed the ax, tossing it aside. He sagged against the wall, watching the guard writhe heavily with pain. Then, stepping over the man, Ruff moved toward the door. There was no point in trying to conceal his work; they would know now.

He kicked one of the new repeaters aside and reached

for the door handle. It slammed open, the snow gusting into the baggage car, and they entered, guns leveled.

"Good evening, Mr. Justice," Gorman Mix said. His collar was turned up against the wind, but those hard eyes glittered as he jabbed Ruff back into the car with the muzzle of his rifle.

The guard was just rising, holding his jaw, and Mix growled at him, "What's the matter, you damned fool? Fall asleep, did you?" His gaze shifted to Ruff Justice. "Not that it matters now."

Clive Colter was beside Mix, and he had a short truncheon in his huge fist. He slapped the club against his palm, his eyes positively glittering. His chin was wet with excitement. The man was literally drooling to get at Ruff.

"Now?" he kept asking. "Now?"

"Hand over your pistol, Justice," Mix told him, and Ruff did so. The hammer on Mix's Spencer was drawn back, and Mix's finger was white against the deadly curve of the trigger. "Now the knife."

Ruff did so, and watched as Mix reached behind him and closed the baggage-car door, shutting out the hard weather. "All right," Mix told Clive. "Now."

6

Clive colter moved in and his vast bulk blocked out Ruff's view of Mix, of the door, of all else. He rolled toward Ruff, his savage little-boy face gleaming with anticipation.

If Ruff stood and waited he would be beaten to a pulp, and he knew it. Yet Mix was waiting with a gun if he should elude Clive. Maybe, he thought fleetingly, the bullet was preferable.

Ruff had no idea of standing there and taking it, however, and rather than wait for Clive to get set, he made his move first.

He took a half-step to the side and then brought up a right hand which had the weight of his shoulders and hips behind it. He caught Clive on the ear with it, a blow which would have sent most men sprawling, their lights out, but Clive shrugged it off.

A stupid grin spread over his face, and he moved in. Ruff batted away a grasping left hand, ducked under a blow from the club, turned over the second stove, and backed into the corner. But Clive kept coming.

Ruff ducked low as Clive swung his club. It shivered the wall at Ruff's back, and he kicked out desperately, trying for Clive's kneecap, wanting to break it into a sack of bony marbles.

But Clive brought him up short. The club slammed down and caught Ruff above the ear. He staggered back, lashing out desperately with boots and fists. His head flashed with lightning and he felt his legs go to rubber.

He connected with a right which landed square on the shelf of Clive's jaw, but now Ruff knew there was nothing behind his punches. That blow on the head had dulled his reflexes, robbed his body of its power.

The truncheon hammered against Ruff's shoulder painfully, and his arm went numb. He covered his face with his good arm, but Clive only laughed, driving the point of the club into Ruff's solar plexus, emptying his lungs. It wasn't going to be quick; Clive didn't want it quick.

As Ruff doubled up with agony, gasping for breath, Clive swung the club against Ruff's hipbone. Exquisitely painful, it sent a tremor of pain through Ruff's already pain-racked body.

Clive grabbed his shirt and brought him upright, throwing him back against the wall of the baggage car. Ruff saw the truncheon raise and with desperate energy threw a short right to Clive's wind, catching him with two knuckles just at the V where Clive's ribs met.

Clive gagged and stepped back, and Ruff kicked him in the face, tearing his nose open. All that was good for was infuriating the grizzly. Clive roared and dove at him, and the truncheon arced through the air, ringing off Ruff's skull.

Ruff struck out, felt his fist drive into Clive's mushy,

blood-warm face, but the truncheon came down again, catching Ruff at the base of the skull, and he went to hands and knees.

Clive hovered over him, bludgeoning him on the spine and then along the ribs. The rib Ruff already believed to be cracked was definitely broken now, and he could only hope that the bone was not jagged, that it did not penetrate his lung.

Not that it mattered much now. Clive was going to kill him with that truncheon if he could. He swung it as hard as he could, striking methodically, viciously, his wind escaping in small grunts with each blow as he put everything he had into it.

Ruff went to his face against the floor, not moving as Clive hammered at him. The only way out was simply to stop resisting, to give it up, and Ruff did.

Clive bounced the truncheon off his head once more and then kicked him in the ribs. If it had been the other side of Ruff's ribcage it would have killed him. As it was it only lifted him from the floor, filling his chest with flaming pain.

He heard Mix's voice as if it came to him through a pail of water. "That's enough, Clive."

"He deserves more," the big man growled.

"Probably," Mix answered casually.

They were talking about something in low, muddled voices which made no sense at all through the haze of Ruff's pain-twisted thoughts. His ribs felt as if they had been crushed, every one, and his left eye was swollen shut, filled with ice. His spine flared up hotly, throbbing, screaming for attention.

Ruff's face lay against the cold floor, something warm and sticky seeping beneath him, and he knew it was his own blood.

He felt massive arms loop around him, felt himself thrown to one side, and then he was bound with wire, the bonds cutting deeply into his agonized flesh. He caught a blur of motion, an echoed, distant voice, and then it was dark and silent in the baggage car.

They rolled on through the storm and the night, rumbling through the long ten-mile tunnel, but Ruff was unaware of it. He was tumbling through his own dark, cold, endless tunnel.

Eventually he saw a flicker of light at the end of that tunnel and he opened his eyes, trying to focus, but the light existed only in his mind. He was still bound hand and foot, his arms and legs numb. It was very dark, very cold, and it was more pleasant just to let the black hole reach up and gobble his consciousness away, and so he did.

He heard low voices, saw a lantern swing away from his face, and he begged them to loosen the wires on his hands.

A blurred face bent to him, and he smelled jasmine. A hand reached out and yanked his head up by the hair, and he heard a woman scream, a faraway sound like the haunting sounds the wind made in the cave dwellings in Arizona—the sounds of tortured souls. The woman screamed again and he thought at first it was Landa. He had stayed with that woman a time, lived with her. It was hot and dusty beneath the cottonwoods in that little adobe house. . . .

His head was slammed back, and then someone roughly untied the wire from his wrists and ankles. The circulation returned with a rush of pain. Pins and needles, nearly agonizing, filled his limbs, and he gasped with the sweet pain of it.

Again someone muttered. He was conscious of the train rumbling beneath his ear, of something dark and crumpled being thrown on the floor beside him. Then the wires were twisted around his wrists again and his head flooded with brilliant crimson and he went under.

It was daylight. Ribbons of light streamed through the cracks above and beneath the baggage-car door. Ruff sat up, or tried to. It was excruciating; a bell rang in his head, his sick and aching muscles cried out with silent grief.

But he managed it the second time, and he sat, his hair across his face, his mind fogged and useless for a minute. He tried to scoot to the wall, to prop himself up, and his legs would not respond. His hand touched something cool and yielding, and Ruff recognized the battered figure of a man for what it was.

Alive, was he? Ruff could not be sure. It was Hargrove, his face swollen and discolored nearly beyond recognition.

Dried blood stained his shirtfront, matted his hair. His scalp was lacerated so badly that it had peeled back like an orange. His eyes were two yellow-blue rubber balls with dark slits drawn across them.

The colonel moaned, and Ruff felt his heart stir with relief.

"Colonel? Colonel!"

He scooted an inch nearer, peering down through his hair at the officer. He thought an eye opened—it was difficult to be sure. A glint of light appeared behind the puffy flesh, and flickered with dull intelligence.

"Who are you?" the colonel moaned. His voice came from deep within his throat. It was throttled and gravelly, rattling like coal down a chute. "Get away. No more!"

"Colonel! It's me. Justice."

"Who?" His head rolled slightly to one side, the curtained eye searching Ruff. "Ruff? Is that you?"

He realized only then that he likely looked as bad as the colonel. His face felt swollen, and it was difficult to speak.

"It's me, colonel. Are you making it?"

"I'm all busted up inside, I think," Hargrove answered. "He got me good, that big one."

"How'd they get on to us, colonel?"

"I don't know. Maybe they were from the start." Hargrove was silent, his breathing labored.

Maybe they had been on to them from the start, but Ruff didn't think so. With a sharp twinge of conscience he wondered if maybe his clumsy work hadn't given it all away.

He slept awhile then, if sleep it could be called. A troubled, turgid sleep in which faces loomed up and disappeared, masked with blood.

Some time later, how long he could not tell, the baggage door opened. He started to sit up and then realized he would be worse off for it.

Two men stood over them, and one commented, "Hell, they'll never make it. Be best for them if we just put a bullet in their heads and dumped them off."

"You could be right. No sense in leaving food for 'em, I guess."

Was that what it was? Some nagging half-realization had gripped Ruff, tearing at his vague consciousness, demanding of him. Now he realized that the insistent demand came from his stomach, and that indeed he was smelling food. Bland, warm food. How long since he had eaten? How long had he been lying here?

He heard them turn to go and wanted to cry out that he was awake, that he wanted food, but something cautioned him against letting them know he was aware of what was going on.

He opened one eye as they left, and from the back he recognized Hurly and Clive. Hurly wore a sling, but he seemed to be moving about easily now. For a brief, vengeful moment, Ruff wished that he had shot to kill in his hotel room.

"Are they gone, Ruff?"

"They are. How are you, sir? Can you sit up?"

"I'm afraid I'd just fall over again." The colonel smiled weakly, and then the sudden realization hit him like a bolt of longed-for light. The colonel was not tied!

"My hands, colonel." Ruff twisted around. "My God, you've got to untie me. I think I'll lose my hands if I don't get this wire off soon."

"I can't," the colonel murmured weakly. For a moment Ruff thought the officer was going to sob.

"Try!"

Ruff scooted nearer to the colonel, and he felt his fingers, like horny claws, rake his wrists. The colonel was panting with the small exertion. He gasped in pain and rolled away. Ruff felt his fingers slide from his wrists.

"Colonel!"

"I can't, Ruff. I'm sorry, but dammit, I can't!"

"You can. You have to, sir. Otherwise we're both dead men, and I'm not ready to shuffle off this mortal coil just yet."

The colonel rolled toward him again, the anguish apparent even on that battered remnant of a face. He felt the fingers grapple with the wire, heard the colonel puffing as he tried to exert the pressure needed to unwind the knots.

He felt something trickling down his wrists, and he knew it for blood—his or the colonel's, perhaps both. And then there was a sudden surge of sensation and his hands tingled vibrantly.

"I think . . ." The colonel gasped and fell away, flat on his back, his chest rising and falling erratically.

"You got it, sir," Ruff told him. Not actually, but it was enough. The wire was loose, and Ruff wriggled free, stripping the flesh from his torn wrists. Finally he had his hands before him.

Discolored, swollen, they seemed unfamiliar, a part of some dead thing. He could hardly control them for a time, and he let them lie against the cold floor, watching them twitch and slowly change from a deep, blotched purple to a healthier brownish-red.

The wire had gouged deep grooves into his wrists, and the wounds were already suppurated. He had come very close to losing them, he guessed, and still might.

That thought sent a surge of anger and determination through Ruff, and he slowly twisted around, finding the ties on his ankles with fumbling fingers. The damage to his feet was not so bad—the wire had been knotted over his boots—but they were numb, as useless as his fingers, which only managed to bloody themselves on the sharp ends of the wire.

Finally he did unwind the wire. He tried to get to his feet, but could not. Slumping to the floor, he rubbed his calves frantically, his eyes on the door of the baggage car.

His gaze shuttled to the colonel; the officer seemed to be out again. "Sir?"

"Ruff? Are you loose?"

"Loose as a goose," Ruff answered. He thought the colonel's smashed lips lifted slightly at that.

"Colonel?"

There was no answer. Ruff half crawled, half dragged himself to the panel on the wall of the baggage car. Someone had replaced the siding, but it was loose. He ripped a board away and removed one of those shiny new Winchesters, continuing to glance at the door.

Then he looked for the cartridges. His hand felt along the floor, searching left and then right.

Gone. The cartridge boxes had been removed.

No one had said Mix was a fool. He sagged against the wall, holding the empty rifle. After a minute he scooted back toward the colonel. Now the old soldier was awake. Not alert, but conscious. He looked like hell, his face pallid beneath the ugly stains of the bruising.

"How did it work, colonel?" Ruff asked, still watching the door, which was bound to open eventually, bound to be filled by a fully fit man with a loaded weapon. And if it happened to be Clive Colter, Ruff would wish for death rather than go through another beating like the last.

"I don't know." The colonel's voice was thin, distant, as if it no longer mattered. "I think Saranevo knew, but they killed him.

"Mix found out about this train, realized that diplomatic immunity extended to the conveyance of the Baroness's party, and somehow managed to get his guns on board."

And there was no doubt as to where those guns were going. Gorman Mix had been supplying the renegades with weapons for nearly two years, always in small batches before this. These weapons would be bound for Stone Eyes, the insane Ute leader. And every rifle in that false wall represented death for innocent people. Stone Eyes was not out to fight a war—as he had boasted, he was out to eliminate the whites, and all Indians who were not Utes, not of his persuasion.

"He must have some hold over the Baroness, or over the vice-premier," Colonel Hargrove said in his whispery voice.

"Blackmail? A business deal?"

"I don't know. The Baroness certainly doesn't need money. I wouldn't think Chapek would either, at least not badly enough to risk international incidents like this."

"Maybe neither of them knew," Ruff suggested. "It could be done. Ankirat? What do you know of the general?"

"Little. He's a hawk, but has no grudge against the Americans that I know of. The same with Zardan. He's chief of their secret police. He's spent time in prison in

France, but he's politically ambiguous; as far as we can determine, Zardan has no reason to lend his weight to anything as small and distant as an American Indian uprising."

"Looks like we blew this one all the way down the line, doesn't it, colonel?" He let his hand rest on the officer's shuddering shoulder. "Well, I got a nice vacation in San Francisco out of it. . . ."

The shoulder had stopped its trembling, and Ruff held his breath, swearing. He let his fingertips search for the pulse in the colonel's throat, but there was none.

Bryson Hargrove was dead. One of Ruff's oldest and closest friends. A good soldier and a good man. He knew Anne Hargrove, and their daughters. A slow anger began building inside of Justice, and the realization that now they must kill him as well.

Someone on this train had murdered an American army officer, and Ruff was witness to it.

He looked down again at the colonel, at his face which was tortured even in death, and then he rose. He got to his feet, although the pain knifed through him from scalp to toes.

He staggered against the wall, but he kept on moving, the useless rifle in his hand. He was going to die—he might as well make it worthwhile.

Above the door the lantern was bracketed to the wall, and Ruff tore it loose. He glanced out the door, finding it barred by two timbers wedged between it and the platform railing. Well then, it was suicide, but it was his life or those of hundreds of others, all probably a deal more innocent than Ruff Justice.

He pulled the stopper from the lamp and splashed kerosene on the wall, on the floor of the baggage car. Then calmly he took his flint and steel from his pocket and struck fire to it.

It went up with a flash, burning a hot red and yellow.

Smoke curled through the room, following the wall to the ceiling, then flowing like a dark liquid across and down, seeking the corners first, then spreading to the floor.

The wall burned quickly, and the smoke grew. Ruff squatted down in the far corner, coughing as the smoke worked into his nostrils, his lungs. He still held the empty Winchester repeater, and he leaned on it, watching with bleak satisfaction as the room was engulfed in smoke and flames.

Tongues of flame reached out and took hold on the crates, the odd pieces of lumber in the car. The Baroness's trunk was wreathed in curling flame, and the smoke was black as sin, strangling.

Ruff choked, closed his eyes, and pressed near the floor. The flames crackled in his ears; the heat was intense. Yet Ruff was able to smile. His head was bowed, his eyes closed. The fire roared in his ears.

Then above the roar of the flames he heard someone shout, and he worked his way over beside the door, watching it through the tears in his eyes, through the rolling smoke.

The door opened and someone started to come in, but he fell back quickly as the fire, drawn by the fresh oxygen, leaped that way, sending tongues of crimson flame toward the snow-lashed platform.

Someone screamed; someone shouted a hurried command; and Ruff knew this was it. His last and only chance, and he took it.

Clive Colter, his eyes wild, appeared in the doorway, and Ruff staggered to his feet, the empty rifle in his hands.

"Get out of my way or I'll kill you, Clive!" he shouted above the angry sounds of the fire.

Appearing out of the smoke like that, he had taken Clive completely by surprise. The big man looked dumbly at Ruff, and Ruff hurried him along, wanting to make his play before the slow intelligence of Clive Colter grasped the idea that the Winchester Ruff Justice held was, had to be, empty.

"Now, Clive!" Ruff roared.

Clive Colter moved aside, turning his head as he choked on the smoke, his massive hands hoisted high above his head.

Ruff clubbed him, wielding the rifle by the barrel like an ax. He hit him as hard as he could, between the shoulder and neck, and the man went down with a thud.

Ruff dragged himself to the doorway, his face being met by a freezing blast of snow-laden wind even as his back felt as if the flesh were roasting off of it.

The soldier who was rushing toward the car had a bucket of water in either hand, but he dropped them, pawing for his holstered pistol. Ruff drove the barrel of the rifle up under the point of the soldier's chin, and the man caved in, collapsing onto the platform.

Ruff grabbed for his pistol, but it slid away on the ice which coated the platform and went over the side. Glancing up, Ruff saw, through the open door of the barracks car, Gorman Mix shoving his way through a knot of confused red-coated soldiers.

There was a pistol in Mix's hand, and he lifted it, his face contorted with rage, but Ruff turned, mounted the railing, and with desperate energy hurled himself off into the shrieking white emptiness of the snowstorm.

He could see nothing of what lay beyond the platform, and a terrifying vision of the vast gorge he had seen earlier flashed through his mind. More likely he would simply bash his brains out against a tree or boulder, but there had been no other choice but to die like a dog under Gorman Mix's guns. And when that is the alternative, no risk seems foolish beside it.

There was only the cold. The white wash of snow.

The wind lifted him slightly for a moment, and then he slammed to the earth, the clacking of the train wheels in his ears, from somewhere seemingly far distant what might have been a shot.

Ruff collided violently with something cold and very solid. The breath rushed out of him and his chest filled with fire. He tried to get up and could not, tried to move his arms and could not, tried to fight his way through the snow and fog of his mind to consciousness, but it was no battle.

The storm swirling through his thoughts was vast and unforgiving. It smothered his consciousness and slowly blanketed it with cold, cold snow.

7

WHEN HE AWOKE it was dark. He wondered if night had fallen or if the fall had damaged his vision. It was cold, and wriggling his fingers, he discovered that he lay in a bank of snow. A small, wind-flagged pine seemed to grow up out of his right side, and he decided that the sapling was what he had hit when he leaped.

He still had a pleasant recollection of the madly flaming baggage car disappearing through the bluish swirl of snow.

He lay there for a long while relishing the thought until the memory altered and became another fire long ago in faraway Virginia, in a faraway war. . . . He realized he was fuzzy around the edges, and with a start considered that he was still lying directly beside the tracks.

If they came back looking, he was dead. Ruff found the strength to lurch to his feet. He stumbled through the unceasing storm, going to his knees in snow with each step.

Something loomed up black and stark against the white veil of snow, and, struggling toward it, he found the edge of a vast pine forest.

He walked on, walking aimlessly through the trees. Here the snow was lighter, but the wind chanted in the boughs and the great pines swayed, rubbing creaking limbs together.

He was walking uphill, and each step was agony. He knew he could not make it much farther, but he wanted to make it as far as possible.

Each additional step improved his chance of survival. The cold was numbing; Ruff was lost in the mad swirl of the storm. His legs moved leadenly but were filled with fire at each step. He knew he could not go much farther, knew that to lie down without shelter would be to die.

He stumbled on, trying to penetrate the snow with his vision, enough to find a shelter of any kind—a cave, a stack of boulders, a crevice. Just a chance.

That was all he wanted now. A chance to live, a chance to track down Gorman Mix and repay him for what he had done to himself and to Bryson Hargrove, for what he had been trying to do to hundreds of Colorado farmers, ranchers, storekeepers, and soldiers. Stone Eyes would kill all in his path, so he had boasted.

To give such a man the means to do it was an unforgivable crime.

He saw it suddenly, and he blinked. A pair of blowndown trees lay across a slight hollow in the ground. There was little snow beneath the twin pines— the patch of bare ground had been what called Ruff's attention to it.

He staggered that way, once falling over a snow-draped rock. After that he could not rise again, but was forced to crawl on until finally, blessedly, he was able to drag himself up under the sheltering trunks of the deadfalls. Curled up in a tight ball, he closed his eyes, listening to the maddened complaint of the storm in the forest around him.

When he awoke, the clouds had parted. The sky was a brilliant blue between stacked, dissipating thunderheads. And they were surrounding him.

The Indians watched him expressionlessly, studied this long-limbed, long-haired, battered man, and said nothing. Ruff struggled to a sitting position and then painfully worked his way out from under the snow-covered trees and stood.

They were Utes. He read it in their broad faces, the square set of their shoulders and chests, the way they cropped their hair. He spoke to them in their own tongue.

"The storm has blown away."

"And left us much snow. And a stranger."

"I'm Ruff Justice," he told the speaker—a thickly built, squat man of forty or so.

"Justice?" another brave interrupted, speaking so rapidly that Ruff could not follow his words.

"He says you are army scout."

"I have been," Ruff said warily. There were six of them, and he was weaponless. If these were Stone Eyes' men it didn't matter if he was army or not. He would be killed for not being one of them. But they were not Stone Eyes' people.

"I rode with army. General Crook," the leader said, tapping his chest. "Fought filthy bad Apache."

"Yes? Maybe I know your name," Ruff suggested.

"I am Ram," he said, puffing up slightly.

"You I have heard of," Ruff lied. "A brave man indeed. I have heard General Crook speak highly of you." The little fabrication pleased the Ute, and Ruff noticed a softening in the expression on their faces.

He was also aware of his legs trembling beneath him,

of a rising sickness in his stomach. He saw Ram nodding at him, saw his lips move, and Ruff attempted a smile before he went face down in the snow.

When he came to he smelled a cooking fire, heard a kid scream with glee, and looking around he saw he was inside a tipi. He had been covered with a warm blanket, and someone with a touch for it had doctored his most severe wounds. There was a salve of some kind, probably bear grease and herbs, on his wrists.

He sat up in bed and started his head to spinning. Ruff lay back for a moment, gathering strength, letting his sleeping body wake up. It was daylight outside, and through a narrow gap in the flap of the tipi he could see rising timber against a backdrop of great purple mountains. Those were the Rockies he was looking at at last.

She came gently into the tipi on moccasined feet, carrying a pot of food and a wooden spoon. She was very young, attractive in a sturdy way, and at the sight of Ruff sitting up she nearly dropped the pot. She backed away, out of the tent.

Ruff smiled to himself. He shifted slightly, bringing pain to his side. But it was a dull throbbing pain and not the jagged white-hot pain of before.

After a few minutes the girl returned. Behind her came Ram. He grinned and nodded with satisfaction as he studied Ruff.

"My daughter says you are awake."

"At last. I apologize, Ram. How long has it been?"

"Two days. At first I thought you died. Then Yarna—that is she—took her medicine bag to you."

"Then I've her to thank. Thank you, Yarna."

She blushed and looked down as he spoke to her. A high-breasted, slim-hipped girl, her face was more delicate than that of many Utes, her nose and lips more finely drawn. She wore her hair in double braids.

"She is a silly thing," Ram apologized with gruff affection. "Every day she brings food to feed you if you are awake. Now she finds you can eat and she runs away to her father."

"I only startled her," Ruff said mildly.

Shyly, with Ram pushing her shoulders, Yarna picked up the food pot and came to where Ruff rested. She sat on the floor, her legs folded under her, and spooned some of the elk stew into a bowl.

When he was finished he returned the bowl to her. "I can eat no more—my stomach is shrunken. But will you tell her it was very good, Ram? And that I appreciate her medicine."

"She understands you," Ram said. "Yarna speaks more English than I have. From a church school. But she is too shy to try it. Yes, Yarna?"

"Yes, Father," she said in a soft voice. Her dark eyes stole only a single glance at Ruff Justice, and then she had gathered up her utensils and rushed away.

"Shy one," Ram said. "A fawn, no?"

"Very like one. I think it can be good in a woman."

"Yes, I too. But only so far, yes?"

"Only so far," Ruff agreed.

"Wait. I have your rifle."

Ram stepped outside and returned with a new Winchester. "It was beside the train road. We saw where you had jumped. Bad business, yes?"

"Very bad, Ram." He noticed the way the man held the repeater and recalled having seen an ancient rifle-musket in Ram's hands the other day. "You keep that rifle, please. Do me an honor."

"If you have enemies, you need a gun, I think, Justice."

"You will shame me if you do not let me repay your kindness, Ram." Ruff smiled, but his eyes were sincere, and Ram nodded with thanks.

"I will keep it, then. But you may not think me a good

friend when I tell you this—you can stay tomorrow, no more. I think you will have a hard travel, but it cannot be helped."

"You are leaving?"

"Yes. Quickly. Very far. Stone Eyes will make a war. He is—"

"I know who he is," Ruff interrupted.

"Then you know why we must leave. No Ute will be presumed innocent when Stone Eyes makes his war. We must be far away. Then when the army has killed the devil, we may come home."

"I can understand that. What you say is probably true. Once the shooting starts, no one will be safe. Many frightened people own guns. They will shoot first and then decide if the dead man was an enemy."

"I believe so. That is the way of war, no, Justice?"

"It is the way of war."

When Ram had gone, Ruff managed to sleep. He was still wounded badly, and the wounds demanded much of his strength. The warm food in his stomach was comforting, and he slept the day away.

When he awoke it was dark and still. A shadow moved near his bed, and he could feel the warmth from her body.

"Yarna?"

The shadow swiveled toward him. "It is Yarna," she replied.

"What are you doing here?"

"Watching over you. If you get a fever it is very bad. And so I watch."

"You should get your rest. You have a long journey ahead of you." She was silent. From far off in the deep forest an owl hooted twice. Ruff saw a thin beam of silver starlight falling through the flap of the tent. The girl scooted nearer to him.

"I do not think I shall go," she said. Her hand fell on

his bed and quickly withdrew as if the bed were hot to the touch.

"If your father goes, you must go."

"I do not wish to leave my home. Why should Stone Eyes force us from our land?"

"Evil disrupts the lives of the innocent, Yarna. You know your father is right."

"But I will stay," she said, her voice solemn and small in the night.

"How will you live?"

"I will live as we always have," she said proudly. Her tiny voice cracked a little with the strain, however. "Perhaps there is a man who will winter with me. A man who needs me for a time."

She was not looking at him, he knew by studying her silhouette, but she did not have to. He recognized her overture for what it was, but he did not respond directly. That would be no way to repay Ram's kindness.

The girl was young, pretty. In another time, some other place, he would have given it serious consideration. But not now, and it was almost with regret that he told her:

"I hope you find such a man. I wish that I could find a woman like you for myself. But I am a warrior, and it is time for me to return to battle."

"Stone Eyes?"

"Stone Eyes is my enemy. There are others. The men who did this to me. I must find them, Yarna, and repay them."

She said nothing else. It was silent in the tipi, and then she was gone. Ruff closed his eyes again. She was only a girl, a girl with a whim, a dream, but for a brief moment there he had wanted her.

Now she would go with Ram and the rest of the tribe; he hoped he had left her with a bit of her dream. He had always despised men who crushed the dreams of young girls.

They roused him at daylight, although he had been long awake. Outside, the camp was active. Horses were being packed, travois loaded with goods. The weather was coming in again, hard off the mountains. Ram was leaving none too soon.

His eyes were dull as well; Ram didn't like leaving his homeland any better than Yarna did, but it was the thing to do.

"I have a gift for you, Ruff Justice," Ram told him as they stood outside the tipi facing the cold wind.

"You need give me nothing, Ram. You have already given me much."

"And you would have me shamed!" Ram said with a smile, "Is that not what you told me—it would shame you to give Ram no gift? Accept my gift in return, Justice. It is only proper."

Proper it was, and the most useful gift Ram could have thought of. A strapping gray horse with three white stockings and a white star on its muzzle, dappled, strong haunches, and a deep, muscular chest. It had to be Ram's best horse, possibly his war pony.

"But it is too much of a gift, Ram," Ruff protested. "Any other horse would do as well."

"Any other horse would be less of a gift. No, this pony is meant for you. You gave me a rifle when you had no other. I have other ponies. Take this one, Justice. You will be well mounted. And if you should meet Stone Eyes," he said in a lowered voice, "do me the honor of riding this pony across his coyote's body."

Slowly then the Utes moved out, riding downward away from the cold of winter and the terror of war. Ram waved a hand in farewell, and Ruff lifted his own in response. He held the gray horse by the hackamore bridle, and the big gray shifted its feet, nodding its head.

It wanted to be with the rest of its kind. Ruff stroked its nose and quieted it.

He could see Yarna's back. She rode a leggy roan, holding herself rigidly, her head straight. He waited for her goodbye, but that never came. Now he waited for her to wave as the Utes disappeared into the snow-covered forest.

But she did not even turn back, and Ruff stepped into the saddle Ram had provided for him. Squinting against the snow glare, he watched the trail where the Utes had entered the forest, and just for a moment he thought he saw her. Small, motionless in the shadows of the big pines.

And then he could see nothing but the winterscape. Nothing but the towering gray clouds drifting off the Rocky Mountain peaks, devouring the blue of the sky. He lifted his hand.

"Goodbye, Yarna," he said softly, and then he turned the big gray, riding eastward toward war.

Ram had put the distance at twenty miles, and it was a tough ride. There were no trails, and the snow was deep upon the mountain slopes. The clouds had roofed over the sky, and a wind rose. Ruff was stiff in the saddle, his body protesting this treatment. He ached leg and shoulder, skull and ribcage.

After six miles he had to get down, and he did so awkwardly, surprising the gray.

He was in a small park on a knoll separated from the mountain by a saddle. He had chosen the spot for its view and its concealment.

Aspen grew in a tight ring around a clearing covered with snow. Above and behind the aspen, now a golden brown, blue spruce thrust up shaggy heads, swaying in the wind.

Ruff walked the horse to the edge of the forest and looked out over the iron-gray and white countryside below. He could not pick out Leadville, but far to the south he saw what might have been the stage station at Dillon. Behind that, Mount Holy Cross loomed, a great pyramidal mountain which was marked distinctly the year round with a cross formed by snow which never melted in deep crevices along the gray flank of the mountain. Just now Holy Cross was completely white, with only dull patches of gray at the foot of the peak.

Ahead was the bulk of the Continental Divide, vast, high, frightening. Mount Elbert stood impassively, nudging the belly of the sky at fourteen thousand feet. To the north lay Tennessee Pass, and beyond that ten-thousand-foot break in the peaks, Leadville and a beautiful woman and a murderous gang of thugs.

"A fair sight, ain't it?"

Ruff turned to find the old trapper standing beside his lead mule, a Sharps rifle in the crook of his arm. He was grizzled, rail-thin, and craggy-faced, but his blue eyes twinkled with merriment.

"It is," Ruff agreed.

"Y'aint plannin' on goin' thataway, are ye? Mr.—"

"Justice. Yes, I am planning on it. Leadville."

"A blight on the mountains," the trapper opined. "It's ragged in the skies," the old man said, squinting at the clouds. "I war over the Tennessee three days back. It's deep, son, mighty deep."

"But you made it."

"I did." He chuckled with amusement. He was looking Ruff over more carefully now, and he had noticed that Justice was unarmed, a rare sight in this country.

"Travelin' light, aren't ye?"

"I have all I need," Ruff told him with a straight face. "I am a child of nature, as we all are." He waved a hand around him. "Nature provides me with all I need, and what have I to fear from nature's children?"

The old man chuckled again, dryly. "You ain't met up

with some of the offspring I have," he said. He spat on the ground.

"Jest in case nature don't provide fer a while, how's for some bacon and coffee? Never did like dinin' alone."

"Under those circumstances, I would be happy to provide company for you."

The old man shook his head, laughing to himself. He went to his pack, removed his cooking utensils and bacon and flour, his rifle never once more than an arm's length from him. He had survived long in the mountains, and care was a habit.

He started a small fire, dumped some used coffee grounds into a blue enameled pot, and started shaving bacon into a black iron pan.

"You came up from Leadville?" Ruff asked as they ate.

"I did. Filthy town, I say. The skies are filled with sulfur from their minin'. Used to be good elk country, now it's populated only by wheeler-dealers, whores, pickpockets, and cardsharps."

"It happens," Ruff commented around a mouthful of bacon and sourdough. "I heard there was Indian trouble."

"Stone Eyes?" The trapper glanced up from his scalding coffee. "He's doin' a lot of braggin', I hear, but not much fightin'."

Ruff's hopes rose slightly. That could mean that the rifles had never gotten through, that the fire had devoured them.

"That's reassuring," Ruff replied.

"Hell, they wouldn't bother no child of nature, would they?" the trapper asked with a grin. He refilled Ruff's coffee cup and began cleaning up, scouring the pan with snow.

"I wouldn't want to find out," Ruff answered with a smile. "But you say Stone Eyes is quiet?"

"I didn't say *that*. He's raggin' all the Utes to take up the war club, shootin' off his boastin' mouth. He's never quiet, Justice, but at least for the time bein' he ain't makin' gun talk.

"Actually I ain't heard much about the man of late. Only news that came down the line was about that there colonel who was supposed to take charge at the garrison in case it did come to a shootin' war. Poor fella was burned alive in a train accident comin' in. Turrible way to go." He shook his head. "What was his name now . . . ?"

"Hargrove. Colonel Bryson Hargrove."

"That's it. You stay in touch for a child of nature, don't you? I only jest heard that day before yestiddy."

"A little bird told me," Ruff said, but he was not smiling. They had managed to explain Hargrove's death handily. That meant there had been no suspicion cast on any of them.

Ruff helped the trapper pack, and the mountain man told him, "Look, mebbe it goes against your religion or somethin', son of nature, but I got me a .36 Remington ree-volver I picked up in a card game. It shoots right and high and the grips are chipped, but it does shoot. Mebbe you'd like to have it—I never did care for no handgun."

"I'd be obliged," Ruff told him. At the smile on the trapper's face, he added, "I can always use it to signal for help."

"I know. I know you wouldn't shoot nobody or no little animules." He dug around in his pack and came up with the Remington.

"I got no extry cartridges. Jest the four that's in there. But then three shots is the trouble signal, ain't it?"

"It is," Ruff said, accepting the pistol with thanks. He took the pistol, checked the loads and the action. Then he tucked it behind his waistband, the cold weight reassuring.

The trapper trailed out, leading his two mules, and Ruff lifted a hand. Then he stepped into the saddle of the big gray horse, aiming it toward the high, snow-clotted Tennessee Pass and the still-distant Leadville.

The snow had begun to fall before he reached the pass, and the wind cut through his buckskins like icy daggers, but he was warm. There was a raging fire riding with him.

8

THE SNOW HAD faltered and died before Ruff hit Leadville, although a dark congress of clouds still deliberated
above the high peaks.

The snow along the main street was trampled to mud
and slush. Planks had been laid across the road at the
corners for pedestrian traffic, but these too were already
covered with reddish mud.

The town seemed deserted as Ruff rode past the mining offices, the general stores, the millinery. But passing
the row of saloons along Front Street he was assaulted
by shrieks of joy, shouts of merriment, and the tinkle of
broken glass.

He counted sixteen saloons in a row along one stretch,
and his eyes caught a half-dressed woman at an upstairs
window. She struck a seductive pose and crooked a finger at Ruff Justice. As he rode on, paying her no attention, she stuck her tongue out.

The Ophir seemed to be the grandest hotel in town.

He noticed it set back from the street on a knoll which had been planted with beech and struggling maple. That would be the place, he decided.

But he rode on a way. The streets now were filled with ore wagons and with mine crews. He spotted a knot of Chinese in black, their long queues wagging as they gabbled.

Up in the hills, yellow-gray smoke rose to blend with the darker skies. He smelled sulfur and heard the constant banging of stamp mills, the chugging of compressors. Leadville was still alive, still stripping the mountains of their wealth. He wondered how long the town would last.

The depot was squat, vaguely red with gingerbread along the eaves. Ruff swung down from the gray and walked into the building.

The small man peered up from behind wire-framed bifocals as Ruff walked to the window beneath the sign "Unclaimed Baggage."

"Yes?" The man's small, upturned nose wrinkled slightly at the sight of the bruised, dirty man in long hair and buckskins.

"I was on Coldwell's private train. I had to detrain briefly, unexpectedly. I was hoping my belongings had been left here."

"Name?"

"Ruff Justice."

"I'll look." He disappeared into the back room, and Ruff stood surveying the train station. Few people were about at this hour. Only a bearded janitor and a drifting cowhand, saddle at his feet.

"You're in luck." The little man had returned. With distaste he placed Ruff's sheepskin on the counter, and as soon as Ruff removed that, he slid the rest of his belongings across. "There is a storage fee, Mr. . . . umm, Justice."

"All right." Ruff leaned against the wall and pulled his boot off. From the boot he dumped a gold eagle, which he handed to the man.

"I'll get your change," he said, holding the coin with two fingers as if fearful of contracting some malady.

The clerk went again into the back room. Johnny Grant was sitting on a trunk, reading the *Policeman's Gazette* with wide-eyed interest.

"Get over to the Ophir," the clerk said, snatching the magazine away from the kid. "Find that Mr. Zardan and tell him Justice has arrived."

The boy got to his feet, tugged his cap down, and waited as the clerk dug a nickel out of his pocket and flipped it to him. Then he was gone with a banging of the door.

"Sorry to be so long," the clerk said, returning to the window. He counted out eighteen dollars and fifty cents, handed it to Ruff, and nodded good day.

Justice held his belongings in front of him across the horse's withers as he rode the short three blocks back to the Ophir. He left his horse with the man in livery and walked into the marble-fronted Ophir.

His room was at the end of a corridor on the second floor, obviously not the best room in the house, but Ruff could not have cared less. It was out of the weather and snug, and it had a bed and a lock on the door.

He stripped and shaved without waiting for the hot water the boy would be bringing up later. Then he dug into his pack and found his little Colt .41 and shoulder holster.

He checked the revolver out and placed it beside him on the table as he lay back naked on the wide bed, studying the ceiling.

After five minutes there was a rap at the door, and Ruff opened it to let the Chinese kid carrying two buckets of steaming water into his room. Three more trips and the curved zinc-plated tub was full enough. Ruff gave the kid a quarter, locked the door and propped a chair under the handle, and then sank into the bliss of the hot tub, his pistol on the floor beside him.

The water soaked away much of the soreness, but Ruff was still stiff, still badly battered. He let his wrists soak in the tub. The water was soothing. He let his head lean back against the tub, and he gently fingered his ribs. They were damned sore; he would have to bandage them tightly before dressing, he decided.

His face, he had noticed when shaving, had almost healed up. There was only the telltale bruising around the right eye, the puffiness on the lips. Yet he had been lucky, very lucky. He thought briefly of Hargrove, who had not been so lucky.

He considered what his course of action ought to be. It was useless to contact the army or the local law. They would find no weapons, assuming they had survived the fire. They were either already in Stone Eyes' hands or stored secretly, awaiting delivery.

There was no evidence as to who had killed Colonel Hargrove. It would be Ruff's word against that of Mix's gang.

Nor was there any point in warning the army that Stone Eyes might soon be hitting the warpath. They had known for months that it was only a matter of time before the Ute warlord started his battle.

There was still something Ruff did not understand about all of this: the Baroness's participation, or Mix's usage of her, whichever it was. The true purpose behind her visit to Colorado . . . maybe it was time to extract the truth from the Baroness Mancek.

He had not forgotten about General Ankirat or about the vice-premier. Either Ankirat or Chapek might be involved in some intrigue, although he couldn't put a handle on what it might be.

Nor had he, for a moment, forgotten about the silent, dark Zardan. He was the dangerous one, this head of the Baroness's secret police. The one who had always been lurking, the one who had kept right on top of Ruff's movements.

He dressed slowly, putting on the dark suit, which was no longer so well pressed. He had an extra white shirt, at least, and it was only a little wrinkled. He positioned the pocket Colt in his shoulder holster and went out, locking the door to his room behind him.

The dining room was lighted with brass chandeliers. Leadville's elite sat at the linen-covered tables discussing mining, politics, and the weather with equal fervor.

Ruff found a table on the raised section at the back of the room, which he guessed was probably a bandstand at special occasions.

A lean, reserved waiter took Ruff's order, and Ruff studied the room. There were bankers, up-and-coming mine owners, gamblers, and one minister, but no one he was looking for.

He ate slowly and sat over coffee while the room changed, people coming and going. The waiter twice sidled up to him, bill in hand, but Ruff ignored him.

The Baroness Sophia dined at eight o'clock in the dining room of the Ophir Hotel. She made a grand entrance, wearing scarlet and diamonds. She had already met a few of Leadville's gentry, and she paused to speak to a man here and there, the general at her shoulder, Chapek and Zardan just behind her.

The waiter preceded her sweep through the dining room. Heads turned to glance at her, and low-voiced comments were exchanged. The waiter held her chair for her, and she started to sit.

Halfway down she saw him and stopped abruptly, then continued awkwardly, plopping into her seat gracelessly. The waiter blinked with surprise, and Zardan's head swiveled.

He was there—or someone so like him. A long-limbed man with waving dark hair and a long mustache sat at a table on a raised platform, sipping his coffee, cool blue eyes on the Baroness, and she gasped, half-rising.

"I've got to see him."

"Who, Baroness?"

"It's Ruff Justice!" A trembling finger lifted to the far table, and the general's eyes followed it. He nearly lost his monocle.

"But . . ." The general could find no appropriate words. The Baroness was already on her feet.

"Don't go," Zardan said.

"Don't be silly, Zardan."

"Then I'll accompany you," the policeman said somberly. He bowed slightly and helped the Baroness from her chair. They walked to where Justice sat stirring his coffee. The Baroness's eyes were open with confusion. Zardan was stone-faced.

"I recommend the pheasant," Ruff said casually. "It's really quite good. They serve broccoli in cheese sauce with it."

"You're alive!" she gasped.

"You're quite right. Undeniably alive. But a little the worse for wear."

"But everyone thought you were dead, that Colonel Hargrove had killed you."

"Is that what everyone thought, Baroness?" Ruff lifted an eyebrow. Zardan had regained his composure, but his eyes were flaming.

"Why, yes. Everyone knew how much he hated you. We thought you two had fought and . . . well, I'm so happy to see you alive. Won't you join us? Tell us about it."

"I've already eaten," Ruff said, standing. "As for talking, we definitely must speak, Baroness. We must speak alone, in privacy." He glanced sharply at Zardan, and she nodded.

"All right. At nine, shall we say? My room—it's 212, at the south end of the corridor."

"I'll be there. You will be alone?"

"Alone?" She hesitated and glanced at her chief of police. "Yes, completely alone."

"Fine. Until later, then." He bent his head to kiss the Baroness's hand, and when he lifted it there was a smile playing on his lips. She responded with a warm smile of her own. Ruff nodded curtly to Zardan and then turned on his heel and crossed the dining room, passing Vice-Premier Chapek and the general without so much as glancing at them.

Sophia watched him go; she felt a sudden pulsing in her throat; her face flushed. Zardan was at her shoulder.

"I cannot approve of this meeting, Baroness. Ruff Justice is a dangerous man."

"Yes," she said abstractedly. "Dangerous and intriguing, Zardan." She touched his arm lightly. "Do not concern yourself. I assure you I can handle him."

Zardan looked once more across the room, watching as Justice disappeared up the stairwell, and he muttered, "I hope so, Baroness. I truly hope so, for your own sake."

Ruff was at her door promptly at nine, but the Baroness was late. He heard her striding up the carpeted hallway behind him, and he turned, enjoying her beauty, the grace with which she moved, the muted invitation in those hips which swayed not more than an inch or two from side to side.

"Am I late?" she asked breathlessly.

"Just in time. I didn't want to start without you, anyway," he said.

"No." She smiled, the tip of her nose turning down. "I wouldn't have wanted you to."

She found the brass key in her red leather purse and opened the door. Her suite was the size of three of his, decorated grandly with twin crystal chandeliers, unlighted now, and embroidered white satin drapes. Matching white chairs sat on the flawlessly polished oak floor.

The Baroness entered the room, locked the door behind them, and fell into his arms. Her scent was enticing, her body demanding as she stood pressed against him, her lips parting, summoning his.

He kissed her and pressed her even more tightly against him, feeling the trembling swell of her breasts. His hand lingered on her hips and his lips touched her throat, her pink, nearly round ear.

"Can you wait a minute, just a minute?" she asked breathlessly.

"Just a minute," Ruff said with a smile.

"I'll change."

She kissed him again and then walked toward the bathroom, unfastening her necklace. Her scent lingered—that faint intriguing scent of jasmine—and it nudged his thoughts.

She had thought him dead, the Baroness had told him. Yet that scent—he recalled one semilucid moment in the baggage car when he had smelled that jasmine powder she wore, when he thought he heard her voice.

If that were so, then the Baroness knew full well that he had not been killed by Colonel Bryson, for Bryson was there, lying badly wounded beside Ruff.

Yet perhaps he was mistaken—he had been half out of his mind much of the time. Perhaps she had been there only in his thoughts. Perhaps it was only a strong desire to see her there, to touch her, to hold her. To see her as she appeared now, returning to the room.

Sophia wore a sheer blue nightgown which accentuated rather than concealed the lush lines of her body.

Her hair was loose; one long strand curled across her milk-white breasts, the rest was draped softly across her shoulders.

She wore an eager smile; her eyes were glazed with sensuous excitement. She stretched out her pale languid arms, and Ruff was to her in two steps. He swept her from her feet and strode into the bedroom, where a single candle burned in a silver holder, and he laid her on the bed.

Her arms and legs were sprawled carelessly like a rag doll dropped against the white satin of the bedspread. She did not move, nor did she speak, as Ruff slowly undraped her form. She simply watched the ceiling, her breath coming more rapidly as Ruff worked his way down, pausing to plant a few warm kisses against her flesh with each button he undid.

When he had the gown open to her feet she lay there like some marvelous, warm creature emerging from the blue cocoon. She stretched out her arms to him now, her fingers making tiny, urgent gestures.

Ruff stood up instead, slowly undressing as his gaze lingered on her breasts, the flow of her hips, the long tapered legs of the Baroness.

Naked he stood there, and she watched him, her eyes nearly closed, her lips parted. He went to her and slipped in beside her, their bodies joining, their lips meeting in a long torrid kiss.

Her hands ran along his spine, up over his buttocks, and down his hard-muscled thighs. She kissed his chest, her hands gripping him tightly.

His hands toyed with her breasts, caressed the soft lines of her hips. "God, you have beautiful breasts," he told her.

"Do you think so?"

He kissed each one. "Yes. Hasn't anyone told you that before?"

"I can't remember anyone before you. If there was someone, I don't know his name, can't recall his face." Her fingers were in his long dark hair, and she smiled blissfully as he traced patterns on her firm abdomen.

"I forget you have had a sheltered life," Ruff told her, kissing her chin.

"Yes. And what about your experiences, Mr. Justice?"

"I've always been painfully shy. Before you, there was only a single quite painful adolescent experience . . . I'd prefer not to talk about it. The scars are deep."

She laughed out loud at the mock melancholy on his face and drew him down against her, snuggling to his body, her mouth eagerly searching his eyes, lips, ears.

Sophia rolled away from him, her fingers lingering on his arm. She lay face down on the white satin spread, her dark hair fanned against the white satin pillow beneath her. Her legs spread slowly as she brought her knees up, her wide, firm ass raising in silent supplication.

Ruff leaned over and kissed the white ivory of her buttocks, and then he scooted behind her, his hands working in circles against her flesh.

Slowly he eased in, and he felt Sophia's hand grasping for him, clutching him with a tiny gasp of pleasure, positioning him, and Ruff drove it home, his thighs against the backs of hers, his pelvis against the soft, upraised cushion of her buttocks.

He held himself against her for a minute, feeling the warmth of her, the rippling of muscle beneath the smooth white skin of the Baroness. Her jaw was slack, her eyes closed.

She continued to toy with him, her fingers caressing his shaft, her own damp warmth, as she drank in the sensuality of the moment. Then, with a tiny expression of satisfaction, her hand fell away and her hips began to rotate slightly, to pitch and roll like a ship on a wild sea.

Her hips drove against him. Ruff had to hold onto her

thighs to prevent her wild movements from disengaging them. She drew out to his length and then shuddered back along his shaft, a small murmur of delight accompanying the end of each stroke as she settled against him.

Her body increased its cadence again, slapping against Ruff. It was an attack, body against body, demanding that Ruff surrender to her; but far from surrendering, he joined in the fleshy combat eagerly, bringing Sophia to a pinnacle at which nerve grated against nerve in a maddening duel which ended in a sudden, shuddering draw.

Sophia writhed beneath him, her body finding a sustained, delicious climax. Ruff leaned forward, grasping at her breasts, biting her smooth shoulder as she trembled beneath him, as he drove himself against and into her time and again, until he too reached a driving, draining climax and he relaxed against her, stroking her flesh, feeling the rustling of her heart, the tiny contractions of her muscles within.

They lay still against the bed. Ruff ran his hands along her sides, her hips, amazed at the flawless skin, the firm toning of the muscle beneath.

She shifted beneath him, and he grimaced.

"What is it, darling?"

"My rib. It's broken, and needs to be tended to."

"My God, you shouldn't be doing this, should you?"

"Probably not. Want to try again?"

She glanced at him with genuine concern. Rolling over, she quickly returned him to his cubbyhole and then, smiling softly, she stroked his cheek.

"I don't want to hurt you, Mr. Justice. I want to take you home and keep you for a pet."

"I bite," he warned her.

She laughed. "I noticed."

"We have to talk, you know." At that Ruff felt an instant rigidity, a dryness.

"Why?"

"Because things have happened which I don't understand. A man was killed."

"But he was nothing to you."

"Bryson Hargrove was my friend," he told her.

She wriggled beneath him now, but it was not a sensuous motion. She was struggling to rise, and Ruff would not let her, not for the moment.

"You don't have to ruin this for me," she complained. "You're hurting me now."

"I've been hurt a little lately, Baroness."

Her face tightened, and she shoved at his shoulders. "Let me up."

"Will we talk about it?"

"Yes, yes, dammit!"

He rolled away and watched as she buttoned her nightgown. He lay on his back, naked still. Now she was not amused by the sight of him.

"Won't you get dressed too?"

"No. Maybe you'll come back after we've talked."

"After this?" Her words were hot, but her eyes were as cold as any Ruff had seen. Still she sat on the bed beside him, resting a hand on his leg.

"You neglected to tell me the whole story when you hired me, Baroness."

"I couldn't. I was frightened."

"Of Mix?"

"Yes, of course! He's a terrible man, Ruff. He really meant to discourage you or kill you that first day in the hotel in San Francisco. He didn't want you working for me."

"Why?"

"Because you are a threat to him."

"But not to you?" he asked.

"You were my only hope." Her dark eyes had softened. Her hand clenched Ruff's leg just above the knee.

"Do you want to tell me now—all of it, Baroness?"

"Yes. What I told you was true, all true in one respect."

"But you said nothing of running guns to hostile Indians."

"That was Mix's bargain. I didn't think you could do anything about that. Not and save Lita too."

"Back to the tale of your sister in the mountain man's hands, are we?"

"It's not a lie!" Sophia said. Amazingly, she flushed. For a woman who was nearly always in control, it was telling.

"Not a lie 'exactly'?" Ruff prompted.

"She's not with Cody MacCormack. That's just a name I heard. I used it to give my story weight." Sophia hesitated, her hands spread in frustration. Her dark eyes suddenly flooded with tears, and her lip trembled. "My God, Justice, don't you see how it was?"

"Tell me."

She took a deep breath and went on. "He came to me in San Francisco. He said there was no point in my going to look for Lita. He had her."

"Had her?"

"Had her hostage. He showed me Lita's ring—the black onyx ring. She was never without it. And there was a note, scrawled on the back of an envelope. It was from Lita, all right.

"Gorman Mix said he had left her with friends, in the mountains. I didn't realize until later that he meant Stone Eyes."

"The Utes have your sister?"

"Yes." Her eyes met his and then shifted away as she asked, "That's very bad, isn't it? I mean, I heard what you and Colonel Hargrove said about Stone Eyes."

"It's very bad," he said.

"I didn't know what to do. I asked him what he wanted."

"And that was to use your diplomatic immunity, to use the private train to haul weapons."

"Yes," she said almost inaudibly.

"And did you really think that would be the end of it, Baroness?"

"What do you mean?"

"Mix is no fool. He knows you have a lot of money."

"I was hoping he would honor his pledge." She nervously fingered her forehead, brushing back an errant strand of dark hair. "The money wouldn't have mattered anyway, as long as we got Lita back. But I didn't trust him entirely. That is why I hired you. I thought that you could follow him . . . do something, I don't know . . ."

She sagged against Ruff, and he petted her dark hair, gripped her shoulder. "He found out immediately, of course. Then, as I say, he meant to discourage you at the St. Regis, but you didn't discourage easily."

"No. I couldn't back out. You see, Gorman Mix's plan was leaked to the army."

"Leaked? Impossible. By whom?"

"By Captain Saranevo. My advertisement was a plant. I was working for the army with Colonel Hargrove."

"Then Saranevo is dead. They killed Hargrove. Tried to kill you."

"And anyone else who got in their way. But Mix succeeded. Those rifles are in Colorado."

"Then there's hope for Lita!" She straightened up suddenly.

"Do you really think so?" Ruff had to ask.

"He wouldn't . . ."

"He's already killed two men. I suppose he could blame it on Stone Eyes."

"I'll offer a reward! A huge reward, one he can't re-
fuse."

"That is exactly what I want you to do, Baroness,"
Ruff said. "Make it an offer he cannot pass up. I want
him to lead me directly to Stone Eyes' camp."

"But you can't go into the mountains now! Alone,
with those renegades up there!"

"I can, and I will. Lita is up there, very frightened and
very alone. And there's a band of Utes who are going to
be well armed, ready to lash out at the world when
spring comes. If I find them now I can prevent all of
that. I will follow him, Baroness, and when the time
comes," he said coldly, "I will kill Gorman Mix."

9

Royal daughters. Enormous wealth.
How does a king live? Contact to discover.

THE ITEM APPEARED in the *Leadville Discoverer* the following morning. It caused people to read it twice, the huge black print standing out boldly. Yet it meant nothing to anyone but the one man who mattered, and Ruff took up a position near the window at the saloon across the street from the Ophir, waiting for Gorman Mix to make his appearance.

Mix was no fool. He had done well enough running guns, selling whiskey, stopping an occasional stagecoach, but what the advertisement promised was wealth to last a lifetime, and a man would have to be insane to pass it up.

Of course, the whole scheme was predicated on Lita's still being alive—something Ruff had kept from mentioning to Sophia.

Lita Mancek's life was dependent on two very violent

and unpredictable men. Assuming Mix would not kill her while there was profit to be made, who was to say what Stone Eyes might do?

The hours passed slowly. Ruff bought one beer which he drank and a second which he did not. He had never cared for alcohol, cared for the way it dulled his senses. He sat in the shadow of the room as dusk fell outside, watching each passing carriage, each horseman.

Of course, Mix might not arrive. He might never see the advertisement, but the way it was being talked about in town a man wouldn't necessarily have to read it to be aware of its promise. Many of Leadville's citizens thought it was a riddle or contest being run by the newspaper.

There were other reasons Mix might not show—if he felt too strongly that it was a trap, he might not come. It could also be, Ruff knew, that despite the threatening weather Mix was even now en route to Stone Eyes' camp to deliver the promised guns.

It could also be that he would not answer the advertisement because Lita Mancek was already dead and Mix knew it. She could have been dead before Mix ever approached the Baroness.

In that case Ruff had blown this case from one end to the other, achieving nothing. The bartender was at Ruff's elbow.

"Are you through, mister? There's some boys would like to use this table for a card game."

Behind the saloonkeeper Ruff saw four men, two of them bearded, anxiously watching. The saloon was busy now, packed with miners, prospectors driven out of the hills by the Indian threat and the threat of a hard winter, gamblers, cowboys, here and there a laughing, painted girl in silk.

"You can freshen this for me," Ruff said, nodding at his beer, which obviously had not been touched.

The bartender started to object, then shrugged. "Tell them they can have the table," Ruff said, "I just want to keep the chair."

"I appreciate it," the bartender said, wiping the badly scored tabletop with a dishrag. "These boys ain't much as cardplayers, but they drink like fish while they're at it."

He turned and waved the group of men over, and Ruff scooted his chair aside a little. They swung extra chairs over and sat down, two of them removing their coats.

"Thanks, partner," the man with the beard said. "Like to sit in?"

"No, thank you. I'm not a gambling man."

Having said that, Ruff had to smile. Not a gambling man—what else could he call this plan? It was one of the longest gambles of his life, and the stakes had never been higher.

He listened to the chatter as the cards were dealt, and was aware of the occasional groans, the low curses, the clatter of poker chips, but his attention was on the street outside, only on the street as the hours slowly passed.

Eventually his patience paid off.

He rode through the dusk-curtained streets with his hat tugged low, his eyes shifting constantly. Gorman Mix rode past the entrance to the Ophir once, then circled back fifteen minutes later.

Ruff watched him patiently, fighting back the savage urge to walk up to Gorman Mix and knock him off that horse. Eventually Mix rode up to the Ophir, which was ablaze with lights now. Some formal function was being held in the ballroom; a local man and his wife had returned from their obligatory European tour, Ruff understood. That was *de rigueur* for Colorado's silver barons, and there were a few of them in Leadville. Many of them made the tour in order to buy furnishings for their mansions, returning with the treasures of Europe to this isolated frontier community.

Gorman Mix was not one of the *nouveaux riches* yet, but he had aspirations.

Ruff glanced at the brass-bound clock above the bar and settled into his chair. It was twenty minutes before Mix returned, and he seemed to be riding higher in the saddle.

Ruff slid toward the door as Mix turned south and up Union Avenue, then he crossed to the hitching rail, stepped into leather, and turned his gray in the same direction.

He let Mix have a good lead; the streets were crowded with miners out for a night's drunk, and Mix didn't even look back. Not that he was that confident, he simply knew that no one dared make a move against him until Lita was safe. With luck, Mix still believed Justice dead. He wondered if Sophia had let his name drop, decided she would not, and shoved the thought away.

Mix rode through the streets, leaving the lighted business district, entering the shadowed, snow-frosted side alleys where rows of miner's tents and hastily thrown-up shacks of tar paper and packing crates jumbled together along the crooked road.

Ruff saw him turn in beside one of these, and he held up his horse, close in to the shadows of a building. He saw Mix walk to the front of the shack, glance around, and enter, faint candlelight from within momentarily illuminating his face.

Now that he had Mix's position, it was time for Ruff to provision himself. He had turned to ride away when he saw, just for a moment, a man scurrying away in the other direction from Mix's shack.

The light was bad and he could not be sure, but it looked for all the world like the cook from the train, the one with the big mustache, Benny.

Ruff frowned. He waited awhile longer and saw the candle extinguished.

From uptown someone cut loose with a rebel yell, and a shot was fired. No one moved in the alley, and Ruff turned away, walking his horse uptown.

He found the emporium open, and he walked in, stamping the mud from his boots before he entered. He picked up a long gun and a new Colt. Cartridges he had aplenty, and the rest of his pack was still intact from San Francisco. He needed only a knife, and could not find exactly what he wanted.

Finally he chose a fourteen-inch Arkansas toothpick with a radically curved blade and a deep blood groove. It was a buffalo skinner's knife and would hold an edge for him, although Ruff preferred having the back side ground down and sharpened as well. He seldom used his knives for eating dinner, and a weapon might as well be as deadly as it could be made.

"That all?" a weary clerk asked.

"It is." Ruff paid him and then asked, "Know where I can buy a good pack animal this time of night?"

"Try the Y-Knot Stable," the clerk said, handing him his change. "But steer clear of Barnaby's next door here. He's got a pot full of worked-out mine mules, not good for a damned thing but poor leather."

Ruff thanked him and went back out into the night. There had been stars earlier, but true to the predictions of the old-timers in the saloon, the clouds were coming in again, and it smelled of snow.

At the Y-Knot, Ruff made a deal for a stubby, deep-chested bay horse and got a pack saddle thrown in. That done, Ruff left Leadville and wound his way up into the denuded foothills. He made camp on the rim of a narrow outcropping, picketing his horses back under the scant trees.

He made a fire and boiled some coffee, all the while

keeping his eyes on the dark square resting among so many other dark squares on the outskirts of Leadville—Gorman Mix's shack. The thunder rumbled in the skies, and from the streets below the growls of hard-drinking, untamed men rose up.

None of it bothered Ruff. He had the quarry in sight, and it was time for the hunt to begin.

At first light the door to the shack opened and a bulky figure in a long gray coat stepped outside to look around. He slapped his arms vigorously, and Ruff guessed it was Clive. Hurly would not be swinging that arm of his like that for a while yet.

Clive leaned one hand against the side of the shack and took care of some morning business, melting some of the snow underfoot in the process. Then he returned to the shack.

After a few minutes Hurly appeared, for the same purpose, and Ruff started his coffee to boiling. Mix was in no hurry; there was no reason for him to be.

He had time to eat and drink two cups of coffee before Mix himself appeared with the Colter brothers in tow. They saddled their horses and tied rolls on behind the saddles.

From time to time Ruff could hear a voice, but they were too far off for the words to be understandable. He squatted on his heels watching them until they turned and rode slowly uptown, trailing through the sloppy, deserted streets.

Ruff rose and walked to his pack. The binoculars had survived the trip from San Francisco intact, and he removed the lens covers, walking back to the edge of the outcropping where the wind gusted over him.

He swept the main street and then a side road, picking up Mix and the Colters as they tied up at a general store where the proprietor was still sweeping up, dressed in a white apron; he seemed surprised to find customers on his doorstep this early in the morning. He returned to his sweeping briefly, but Mix waved an impatient arm and Ruff saw the storekeeper go inside, followed by the three men.

In fifteen minutes they were back, carrying gunnysacks, which they slung over the pommels of their saddles. They rode out of town at the north end, and Ruff watched them for only a minute longer before lowering the glasses and putting them away.

He saddled without haste. He had no fear of losing their trail, not in this snow. There were only so many passes, and now he knew which one Mix would use.

His fear of being seen on their backtrail was much greater. He would move with caution, keeping well back and staying in the timber when possible.

Once the Mix gang had altitude, it would be an easy task to pick off a following rider with a rifle. And not for one minute did Ruff forget that wherever Mix's trail ended that of Stone Eyes would begin.

They had a good mile on him when Ruff swung down onto the snow-heavy flats north of town and began to parallel their trail.

The wind was rising, the day darkening, and Ruff slipped on his sheepskin as he rode, buttoning it to the throat. He rode with his Henry repeater across the saddlebows, always ready, and his eyes alert to the shifting shadows cast by the trees and the low running clouds.

Yet he did not then notice the other man, the man on his backtrail. Zardan had waited patiently in the empty stable at the edge of town, watching as Mix and the Colter brothers rode out. Then he lit a cigar and leaned back against the scalloped, weathered partition behind him and waited.

After an hour or so, Justice appeared, as Zardan knew he would. Zardan watched him with narrowed eyes, and after Justice had disappeared into the timber across the flats, he buttoned up his fur coat and stubbed his cigar out. Then Zardan too mounted his horse and followed that hard trail into the high country.

It was three hours to the abandoned farm, and Ruff drew up in the shelter of the tall pines, watching as Mix led his small party across the meadow studded with stumps to the dilapidated old ranch house.

Mix swung down and walked to the door, rapping on it. He turned his back, crossing his arms, rocking on his toes. Finally a man appeared in the doorway—a big man wearing red long johns above homespun pants—and Mix went in, leaving the Colters with the horses.

After a while they emerged from the house, the big man now wearing a buffalo coat. A second man followed, and the three of them tramped around the side of the house.

Ruff settled in to wait. An angry jay hopped from branch to branch overhead, scolding him. The clouds across the long meadow were stacked into the shape of a horse's head. Black, nearly blue, they were laden with lightning and hard weather. The mountain peaks to the west were obscured by tiered, flat-bottomed clouds.

The men returned leading three mules; each mule carried two long packs. It took no imagination to guess what they contained.

One of the men ducked back into the house, and then they trailed out, crossing the meadow and a small, icy rill before entering the blue spruce forest on the far side.

Ruff rode after them through the darkening day. The wind was stirring now, shuffling the ranks of snow-heavy spruce and cedar. The world was strangely lighted, electrical, and from time to time ivory-white lightning arced overhead.

A tree, lightning-struck at its tip, smoldered and sputtered as Ruff wound through the wet trees, keeping half a mile north of Mix's party.

It had begun to snow lightly when darkness fell. From a low ridge Ruff could see the red flickering of Mix's campfire. He could afford the luxury—after all, he had nothing to fear from the renegades. Ruff could not.

He huddled beneath the cedars, watching the wind drift the snow across the deep valley below him, gnawing on cold biscuits, drinking cold coffee as the heavy clouds snuffed out the day.

He was alert, on edge, but not particularly worried—Mix had not seen him, he was sure. And Stone Eyes would be deep in the mountains yet. He hadn't yet received the rifles which would make him bold.

Only once did Ruff feel that something was not right. It was just before dark when the shifting light bled purple and blue across the white snows, when the drifting clouds mottled the earth. Just for a moment he thought he had seen something—light on metal, on glass, a brilliant reflection where none should have been. But it was probably nothing. An errant ray of sunlight on a bit of mica, on standing water or ice. He watched the area closely for long minutes and then shrugged it off, deciding that he was as susceptible as any man to a case of nerves.

10

THERE WAS A break in the snow at daylight. The sun
formed a brilliant golden fan through the clouds. It was
cold; the horses stood with heads bowed, eyeing the men
miserably.

Gorman Mix had the fire going, the coffee boiling. Big
Sam Dawkins and his son were loading the mules, Hurly
was just rolling out. Clive still slept like a dark lump
against the white of the snow.

Mix prodded him with the sharp toe of his boot, and
the big man groaned, peering with one eye at the dark,
scornful face of Gorman Mix.

"Get your butt out of that sack, Clive," Mix growled.
Then he turned to trudge back toward the fire, which
flickered dully in the center of a melted clearing.

"Long ways to go today," Hurly ventured. He held
his cup in his left hand. His right was still not that good.

"What makes you think so?" Gorman Mix snapped.

"Well . . ." Hurly half turned toward the high pass

beyond the virgin forest. "Stone Eyes' camp is six miles beyond that, ain't it?"

"We're not going to Stone Eyes' camp."

"We're not?" Hurly blinked dully.

"Of course not. Use your head, Hurly." Mix squatted on his haunches, holding his palms out to the fire. "It's a new game now. The deal I made with that Baroness."

"Stone Eyes still wants his guns."

Gorman Mix spat and shook his head. How had he ever gotten hooked up with two imbeciles like the Colters? When this was done it was adios time.

"He'll get his rifles," Mix explained. "The thing is, I want that girl back. I told him he could keep her, use her. Now I want her back."

"You gonna make a trade?"

"That's right," Gorman Mix said. He watched as Sam Dawkins walked through the snow toward them. "The thing is, Hurly, I'm not walking into Stone Eyes' camp to do my trading. I don't trust him no more'n he trusts me. He'd likely turn those guns on us just to test 'em out a little."

"You're right," Hurly said, the idea obviously a new one to him. "So what're you gonna do?"

"I've got it worked out. We'll meet on neutral ground. He can bring the girl and his gold and two braves—no more. We'll make the exchange, and then the son of a bitch can do whatever he wants to. Me, I'll be long out of Colorado."

Hurley chuckled. "You're a clever one, Gorman."

Mix ignored the compliment. He rose, taking Sam Dawkins aside. "How far is that cabin?" Mix wanted to know.

"Six miles," Dawkins said. He was a slow-talking man who spat out each word grudgingly as if it cost him. He lifted a finger instead of bothering to tell Mix where the deserted cabin lay.

"About noon, then, if we don't get hard weather."

" 'Bout," Dawkins agreed. His son, a man of the same stamp as Dawkins, had come up, but he stood ten feet away respectfully. " 'Bout three I'll make the Injun camp."

"Let's get it moving, then," Mix told them all. "I don't like the feel of this weather, and I don't aim to be here when it starts up." They were at eight thousand feet now and the peaks loomed high above them. By noon they would have climbed another thousand feet, and much of that was along a broken, treacherous mountain trail abandoned when the shoestring silver mine along Little Sandy Creek had been abandoned.

"I ain't et yet," Clive Colter complained solemnly. He was still tucking in his shirt.

"Eat later, Clive," Mix said in exasperation. "Eat yourself to death if you want when this is done. For now, let's ride."

Sullenly Clive saddled his big roan and climbed into the stirrups. They trailed out westward, Dawkins leading the way, Mix riding last as he always did. Gorman had lived a long time on the outlaw trail and he had some cautious habits. He let no man ride behind him.

From the timbered slope of the hill to the north, Ruff Justice watched the party through his binoculars. He stayed well back among the pines, keeping the sun from his lenses.

He watched them for most of an hour, puzzled when the gang angled northward and entered Dead Cow Gorge. There were a dozen easier routes through the mountains. That trail was up along stony cliffs with a drop of thousands of feet to Little Sandy, which would be raging just now.

There was nothing on the surface of this that figured. What was up Dead Cow? He could only recall the old

Stanford Silver Mine, but the Stanford had been shut down for years.

Then, slowly, understanding came. The man was trying to outfox the fox. Mix wanted to make an exchange and get out with his skin. There were some old buildings up at the Stanford, mostly dilapidated, but the old mine office was of stone and would have fared a little better.

Ruff put his glasses away and waited. He let them enter the gorge, knowing now where they were going. To follow closely was dangerous. Once at the Stanford they would certainly keep a guard posted, and it would be hard to approach.

From what Ruff remembered, the stone cabin which had served briefly as the mine office sat on a knoll that had been cleared of trees—trees being only a nuisance to a mining operation—and was littered with shale and slag, residue of the work which had gone on furiously for about seven months before the vein Stanford had been so eagerly following simply dead-ended. "Meeting a horse," they called that; finding that the upheaval which had forced the silver to the surface in the first place had also deposited huge stone formations—horses—along the vein.

Stanford had been the only man to think there was any point in trying to go on with the operation, and the Utes had gotten him. At least they believed it was Stanford—there was hardly enough left to be certain.

Ruff climbed into the saddle, holding the gray back for a minute. He looked to the north and then to the west. He had never heard of a back way over Prospector Peak into the area of the Stanford, but he meant to find one.

To ride up the gorge was to ride into the guns of Gorman Mix. If the weather did not set in, he thought he could circle Prospector and come up unseen on the old mine from the north.

He looked to the shadowed, barren pinnacle of Prospector. It was a bad risk, but the best he had. Slowly Ruff turned the gray northward through the timber, leading his pack horse. Thunder rumbled through the skies, shaking the earth and the snows began again.

Her head came up at the sound of English being spoken, and she felt herself begin to tremble with faint hope. The big woman who sat watching Lita pushed her down as she tried to rise.

The Ute squaw went to the flap of the tent and peered out, and Lita caught a glimpse of the savage face of Stone Eyes. He was speaking to a big man in a buffalo coat, a man Lita had never seen before. Stone Eyes was very angry, and the big American simply shrugged or commented from time to time, "I cain't he'p it. It's not my show."

"Mix is a coward, a liar."

"The weather's hard—he don't want to risk comin' in," Dawkins replied.

"You are here."

Dawkins only shrugged, and Stone Eyes glowered at him, the tendons on his strong neck standing taut with anger.

"I want my guns!"

"He'll give 'em to you. I told you where."

Stone Eyes was enraged. For a bloodthirsty moment he was inclined to cut this messenger's throat and ride with his entire band down to the old mine. Yet that would be a difficult battle. His braves were still armed with inferior muzzle-loaders. He forced himself to calm down. The snow drifted between the two men's faces. Across the camp, smoke rose from a fire where three women smoked venison against the hard winter which was coming on.

Stone Eyes shrugged finally, as if it made no difference to him. He had his rage under control now. "All right," he said calmly. His brain still hummed with residual anger.

Stone Eyes' anger was terrible to behold. He went completely out of his senses when it came on him. It was an uncontrolled, self-destructive thing. He had been this way all of his life—it was why he was no longer welcome in most Ute lodges. He had been known to sit talking peacefully for hours until a remark, a look, an imagined slight sparked him. Then he was utterly wild, reaching for the nearest weapon, using bare hands if necessary to smother the life from his imagined enemy.

The spirits walked with Stone Eyes at times. In the dead of night he heard voices; always they told him the same thing: "Kill. Cause blood to run; appease us with crimson fire."

And Stone Eyes had followed these directives with a vengeance. In a violent frenzy he had killed until the snow bled, until the lodges of his enemies were painted with gore, until his own hands were red, his body steaming with their sacrificial blood. He had killed and would kill until blood flowed across the land, stained the rising grass, until there was blood in the rivers and blood on the moon.

To accomplish that he needed Mix's new repeating rifles, and he knew it.

"All right," he panted, "tell Mix I will come and bring the girl."

Lita felt her heart leap. The man was from Gorman Mix, and there would be some sort of exchange.

She hated Mix. He was a crude, vicious man. When he had taken her from the hunting camp he had cold-bloodedly killed Howard Trammel, her guide.

But at least Mix was human. Stone Eyes was a demon. The sight of him was enough to turn her stomach. The way he looked at her—she knew where he had gotten that name. Those cold, awful eyes that should have belonged to some wild animal, not to a human being.

She awoke one night to find him standing over her, naked in the darkness. Simply standing there for nearly an hour as Lita cried and trembled. Then the Ute had turned and walked out without touching her. But she could never sleep after that, knowing that he would return on another night, not knowing what he would do.

She loathed Mix, yet she would be away from Stone Eyes. Anything was preferable, and she decided logically that if Mix wanted her it was for some reason—perhaps her father had paid him for her; perhaps the American authorities had demanded her return.

The door to the lodge flapped open. Stone Eyes stood there, massive, a habitual cruel expression on his scarred face. He was bare-chested despite the snow Lita could see falling behind him.

"Dress. We are traveling."

She obediently, hastily did as she was told. Stone Eyes watched every movement she made, and for a moment she thought she saw a dull, savage thought flicker behind those black, hard eyes, and her breath caught. But he turned moments later and went out, calling to some of his men.

Lita pulled on and buttoned her boots and slipped into the warm, ermine-lined coat she had purchased that terrible winter in Moscow. Then she stood silently, a small, unsteady figure in the corner of Stone Eyes' lodge, hoping against hope that her life would not end in these desolate mountains, that somehow sunshine and wine, spring flowers and peaceful days might come again.

Ruff Justice wished for much the same. The snow blew like the banshees out of a frozen hell as he crossed the high, barren divide. The horses' tails were blown up over their backs, and the wind was strong enough to shove Justice along, twice forcing him to his knees.

Panting heavily, the breaths he took like ice in his tortured lungs, he surveyed the long gorge beneath him. The snow was blowing nearly horizontally, and it was increasingly heavy. He could not make out the cabin and wondered if somehow he had lost his way.

The gorge was gray rock and snow, treeless except for a few stunted pines deep in the valley along the white-water frenzy of the creek which frothed and roared its way along its winding channel, moving boulders and uprooting young trees on its banks.

The sun was a leaden ball behind a screen of clouds, and it rested low in the sky. Looking down the ice-slick, granite slopes, Ruff doubted a man or a horse could make it at night without breaking a leg or worse.

There were no trails, just a steep, icy declivity which ended at a sheer cliff face which fell for a hundred feet—perhaps more, he could not see from where he stood—and then more barren mountain, here littered with shale and huge snow-dusted boulders.

Timberline was another thousand feet. Ruff would have to be in the open for nearly half a mile or take the risk of trying it at night. Probably a more hazardous choice than leaving himself open to snipers.

How long did he have? There was no telling. Had he guessed right that Mix would be exchanging the guns for Lita? Would Stone Eyes agree? He hunched his shoulders against the bite of the wind, realizing he had no answers to any of the hundred questions he could ask of himself right then. He could not even answer the basic question—what kind of a fool of a man attempts such tasks? What sort of man was Ruff Justice after all? His thoughts broke off.

There it was. And then it was gone. Across the canyon on the opposite peak at about his altitude. He had seen movement, was sure he had seen movement, and it worried him.

He watched silently for long minutes, searching the distant peak carefully, foot by foot, but he did not see it again. Yet this time he had no doubt—someone was over there, which added yet another question to his lengthy list. Who was there fool enough besides himself to be out under such conditions? He did not consider it likely that it was a friend. It worried him, puzzled him, but it decided him.

He would not attempt it in daylight. Ruff loosened the cinches on his horses and settled down, his back to the driving wind, the mounting fury of the storm, to wait for nightfall.

11

WHEN IT WAS full dark, Ruff Justice rose and removed the saddles and bridles from his two horses. There was no way on earth they were going to make it down that icy slide. This way they would have a chance. If they had good instincts they would follow the trail back toward Leadville and find themselves back in the familiar, warm stable in two days.

What his own chances were of getting out of the mountains without horses, Ruff did not care to calculate.

He made a small pack up, wrapping food, ammunition, rope, and binoculars in a blanket which he tied with a piggin string and lashed to his belt. Then, looking briefly to the cold, soot-black skies, he moved out.

The footing was treacherous, ice and cold stone. Once when the moon shook itself free from the strangling clouds he watched the mountain shimmer like silver—a sight that would have filled old Stanford's heart with joy—but it was only ice.

Ice draped over the mountain like a cruel, cold winding sheet, glittering hard and silver beneath the silver moon.

Ruff worked his way downward cautiously. Somewhere ahead the mountain fell away dramatically, and to slide over was to die.

He got to a sitting position, the only way to move across the vast sheets of ice glazing the peak, and slid forward, tearing the flesh from his hands, groping for outcroppings to slow his progress when it got too fast.

At one point he found himself sliding at a tremendous speed across the silver sheen of ice with no hope of stopping, the surface beneath him as slick and polished as cold glass. There was nothing on the land, no tree or rock or brush—nothing could survive long at this altitude. There was only Justice skidding madly down the face of the mountain, down the long silvery chute toward the dark chasm below.

Gradually the angle of the slope decreased and he slowed, but he had broken out in a cold sweat. He stood in the second attempt and inched toward the edge of the precipice, his breath steaming against the night.

There seemed to be no way down, and he paced the rim, eyes straining. Earlier he thought he had detected a ribbon of a trail, perhaps an ancient Indian road, but with the vanished daylight the trail had disappeared.

It was doubly maddening because now he could see, down the valley, a light from the old mine and a ribbon of silver smoke twisting into the skies.

He walked as far as he dared to one side and then back. Still he saw nothing. He could go no farther in either direction. He stood now on a broad ledge of granite which was broken away at either end by avalanches. The snow was thirty feet deep in the cuts, and there was no hope of making it alive. The only hope was downward.

Turning to look back up the mountain, Justice even doubted if he could return the way he had come. No, it was down or nothing. And there was a trail, had to be!

Of course, he had viewed it from far above, and there was every chance he had been mistaken. The trail might not come within fifty feet of the rim. The mountain was old and the trail nearly as ancient. If trail there was, it had likely been used ages ago by the one the Indians themselves called "the-ones-that-came-before." The ancients. Did their ghosts still haunt the sacred mountains, still protect their secrets? Did the ancients provide illusions to mystify and ensnare interlopers?

Again he searched. And then he saw it. The trail, appearing like a gray line sketched against the darker gray of the cliff, gleamed dully in the feeble moonlight. It was a good seventy feet straight down.

The ancient trail had crumbled off, defeated by time and the elements. It was exceedingly narrow at this end as well, and Ruff threw his head back, taking a deep breath. Slowly he breathed out, letting a soft curse go with his breath.

It was the only way, and so there was no sense in debating whether to try it or not. The problem to be resolved was how.

Casting about, Ruff found what he wanted—what appeared to be a loose boulder beneath a mantle of snow was actually a rounded projection of harder granite which had decomposed at a slower rate than the soft material around it.

Ruff formed a loop with his rope and tied on, testing the outcropping for strength. Again he walked to the rim of the mountain. Now the trail was invisible again— the moon slid behind the clouds and the night grew darker still.

He knew where it was, though. Straight down. Justice rolled his hat and stuffed it into his hip pocket, then he drew his gloves on tightly. He hesitated a minute, and then, with his rifle slung over his back, he stepped off into space.

The cliff face beneath the rim angled back sharply, and as Ruff made his first move he instantly felt the earth fall away from his feet. He felt the rope tear at his hands, and he grimaced with effort.

The wind buffeted his body, turning him and lifting him as he slowly descended. Snow from the ledge fell free and sifted over him, bringing with it a fist-sized rock which bounded painfully off Ruff's shoulder.

Down he went, into the black chasm, the shrieking of wind in his ears. He measured his descent roughly as he went. That was a hundred feet of hemp rope he had, and his eye had always been fair at measuring. He hoped it had been this time.

It was pitch black now, the wind toying with him; his hair drifted across his face; his arms were leaden, the sockets fiery.

His searching boots found the face of the cliff once more and he was able to brace himself against the hard wind, but now Ruff was growing worried. He could feel how much slack he had left, and it was not much.

Maybe his eye was not that good anymore. If he came up short, there was no way he could climb that icy rope a hundred feet in these conditions, and the only way to go then was down. Straight down and quickly.

His boot toe, pawing at the cliff, finally made contact with a lip of stone, or what seemed to be. He paused, panting wildly, his eyes peering into the darkness, trying to make out the form of the trail.

There was a ledge there, of that he was sure. But if it was not the end of the broken trail, he would sit on that ledge until he died.

His hands were frozen, the rope icy, and Ruff felt

himself starting to slide away from the ledge. He had to make a decision and make it now.

He pushed off with his feet and swung back. When both feet touched flat, he let go of the rope, lurched forward, and sprawled, trying for a grip.

But the surface was icy and narrow, and he had rolled halfway off the ledge before he found a grip and pulled himself up onto it, his heart pounding like thunder.

The night was bitter cold. The wind screamed through the canyons, drifting snow. Below he could make out nothing but the white froth of the raging river against the darkness.

Ruff Justice sat on a ledge on the side of a barren icy mountain with no way up and only a treacherous, broken trail no wider than the span of two hands down.

And what if the trail was broken off at another point? Covered by a slide?

He smiled at himself, knowing he had worked himself into a fine corner and only dumb luck was on his side.

It was cold on the ledge, and to remain still was to freeze. Ruff got to his feet, pressing his face and chest against the cold wall of the mountain, embracing its icy face like a baby suckling.

He moved downward, his foot inching ahead, testing the solidity of the crumbled stone. Rocks and debris he kicked off ahead of him. It was painfully slow, and his face and hands were numb within half an hour. His feet had long ago lost any warmth.

He moved on now because it was all there was to do. It seemed as if his entire lifetime had been spent on this mountain trail, searching for fingerholds, pressing his face to the raw stone.

And then he came to the slide.

His foot met the rockslide, and he knew instantly he was in deep trouble. Stretching out his hand, he found tons of debris and ice completely blocking the trail, and he leaned his head against the cliff, trying to pull himself together.

How wide it was, how solid, he did not know. It angled out into space, the end of the slide truncated by gravity. He glanced down nonsensically—Ruff already knew what lay below. Empty, dark space.

What now? Go back and climb the icy rope a hundred feet, renegotiate the ice slide, walk out to Leadville in hard weather? Not likely.

The only way was onward . . . or downward. Ruff fingered the slide and dislodged a few stones, which clattered away. When he had found a firmly imbedded rock he could grip he crawled onto the slide, his pulse pounding in his temples. He moved inches at a time, hugging the loose debris, knowing the whole thing could simply fall away beneath him. And he would have time on the way down to think of all the mistakes he had made in his mad life.

His foot found a stone, and he put his weight on it. But when he shifted it fell away, and Ruff clawed for a grip. He had slipped down now, nearly off the trail, and he had to crawl back up.

Now he could see that the slide was no more than twenty feet wide, and he believed he could make it. He moved slowly, not trusting his weight to any single object. And then he was across, standing trembling on the trail.

He rounded a bend, and the trail widened to nearly thirty inches. Still he moved ahead cautiously, alert for the tricks of the gusting wind, the ice underfoot.

Once he found a gap in the path some ten feet wide, and he had to leap it. But at least the stone stayed put, and it was simple compared to jumping between moving railroad cars.

He moved on steadily now, the moonlight holding for half an hour, the trail gradually widening and flattening until at last he was down among the pines, on the floor of Dead Cow Gorge, half a mile from the stone cabin where Mix awaited the arrival of the Ute butcher.

He formed his hat, caught his breath, and unslung his rifle. Then, stealthily, his footsteps covered by the roar of the white water river beside him, beyond the pines, he walked toward the Stanford and the savage guns.

He came upon it suddenly. The forest fell away, and across the cleared ground he saw the cabin, dimly lighted. He could see only a single high, narrow window. Crouching, he heard nothing, and then he did—a mule brayed from off to his left about a hundred yards distant.

His eyes studied the cliff face there. It was the entrance to the old Number Two Stanford, he thought, and as he searched the mountain he picked out the dark cut against the gray stone.

They had their mules and horses in there, sheltered from the weather. What else was in there? Who else?

Stealthily Ruff circled back through the pines, reaching the base of the cliff a hundred feet from the entrance to the old mine. Working his way along the foot of the mountain, rifle in hand, he worked toward it.

Ice crackled underfoot, but the river beyond drowned out all such small noises. It was utterly black now, the moon having surrendered to the mass of clouds. He heard an uncomfortable mule shift its feet and then quite suddenly saw a light.

The light appeared and then as suddenly disappeared. A moving light meant a man, and Ruff fell back against the cliff, holding his rifle to his chest.

Easing toward it, he now saw the mouth of the mine tunnel painted with yellow, wavering light, and he peered in.

Hurly Colter sat in brooding silence on a rock, a blanket wrapped around his huge shoulders. He was staring directly at Ruff, but because of the lanternlight in his eyes and the darkness outside, he never saw him. At least Justice thought he hadn't.

He waited a moment, his Henry cocked and ready, but there was no cry of alarm and Hurly did not appear. He had seen them—just over Hurly's shoulder. Six long crates ready for delivery to the man who wanted to make this territory run red.

How much time was there before Stone Eyes appeared? Very little, Ruff guessed. Something had to be done now, and he waited until the mule brayed again. Then, figuring that Hurly would automatically glance that way, Ruff stepped into the entranceway, behind the massive Hurly Colter.

"Hurly?" he said softly.

"What?" Hurly's eyes opened wide, but he didn't get the chance to say anything else before the stock of Ruff's Henry repeater slammed into his skull, knocking him against the floor, where he lay peacefully, eyes shut.

He dragged Hurly back farther into the mine shaft, the mules pricking their ears with curiosity, at the sight. He bound Hurly with his belt and gagged him with his own scarf. Leaving him strapped to a timber, Ruff returned to the mine entrance. He turned the lamp out and stood, letting his eyes adjust to the darkness.

Now it got a little tricky. His instincts told him to destroy those rifles, but cool logic argued that Stone Eyes might hold the girl until he had examined the guns. To remove the rifles might be to risk Lita's life.

How long before the Utes arrived? How long before Hurly was scheduled to be relieved?

Ruff slipped out of the mine shaft and worked toward the back of the stone cabin. There were no windows on the backside and he made it without trouble.

Working toward the side of the house, he found an

old barrel, and he propped it up, chinning himself to peer into the high, narrow window.

Gorman Mix was there, feet propped up on a crate, the fire behind him flickering on his savage face. He was speaking to someone, and from the slow response, Ruff recognized Clive Colter.

Where were the others? The man in the buffalo coat and the kid? Someone would have had to ride to the Ute camp, unless this was prearranged, which Ruff doubted. And one man posted guard. That accounted for all of them. Naturally the newcomers had the dirty jobs—riding to disappoint Stone Eyes and standing guard down that windswept canyon.

"Damn near . . . if the son of a bitch hasn't killed Dawkins," he heard Gorman Mix say. Clive mumbled something in return.

"Just keep your pants on. We'll be gone soon."

Ruff dropped to the ground. The barrel toppled over, and he froze. But no one appeared. The wind and the river had covered the sound. The stone walls of the cabin had muffled it.

He returned to the mine-shaft entrance. He knew now that Mix expected Stone Eyes soon. If he knew Mix, the Ute would be allowed to bring only a few warriors. And if he knew Stone Eyes, there would be more Indians up in the mountains, watching.

Any number added to Mix's force would be too many for Ruff to handle alone, and he knew it.

"You've got this all worked out now, don't you Justice," he muttered to himself. "All that's left to do is haul away six crates of rifles, rescue the girl, fight off a dozen armed men, and make your triumphant escape out of here through a blizzard."

He sat down on Hurly's vacated rock to do some serious thinking.

12

◄──◆──►

RUFF JUSTICE WAITED in the darkness, holding the mules, which he had hitched together. The snow had begun to fall again, and he could barely make out the mine entrance, which was only twenty feet away, nor could he clearly see the outlines of the stone cabin.

Hurly was resting peacefully in the rocks, the snow settling over his bulky body. Stone Eyes had not yet come, and there was nothing to do but be patient. He kept his gun hand warm, holding it against his bare stomach, and waited. All hell was going to break loose soon, and Ruff was not sure if he dreaded it or welcomed it. At least something decisive would happen—that much he knew, and if it carried the heavy risk of death at least it offered the simultaneous chance for life for Lita Mancek and hundreds of others in Colorado.

He waited, crouched beside the mules. The night grew darker, colder, although it seemed hardly possible. His legs grew stiff. Hurly moaned from the rocks, and still Ruff waited.

Suddenly they were there.

They came from out of the gloom of night as silent as dark specters. They were illuminated starkly by the wedge of light which fell through the cabin door as Gorman Mix opened it and stepped out to greet his partner in crime, his enemy, Stone Eyes.

"Welcome, Stone Eyes," Ruff heard Mix say. Stone Eyes answered sharply.

"I do not want your welcome. You are a liar, Mix, a trickster."

"I'm only watching out for my own hide," Mix answered with a short laugh. His eyes lifted to the snow-screened hills beyond. "How many wild cards you got thrown in?"

"Wild cards?"

"Never mind. What do you think, Dawkins?" Mix asked the big man, who only now emerged from the snow clearly enough for Justice to make him out.

"I didn' see no other Injuns—'course that don't mean a whole lot, I guess."

"What is this delay, Mix? Another trick?" Stone Eyes demanded. "Have you the rifles?"

"Have you brought the girl?"

"I have. She stays across the river until I have seen the weapons."

"No deal," Mix said strongly. "Let's have a look at her."

Stone Eyes let his gaze rake Mix's wolfish face, and then he turned slightly and said something hurried, sullen, to the warrior beside him.

The Ute nodded and rode back into the snow. They were all silent. Ruff heard nothing but the wind until the warrior returned, leading a paint pony.

She sat there, cold, trembling, slight. Her face was

screened by snow and her own dark hair. She wore a fur
coat, her hands were tied to the saddlehorn. But Lita
Mancek's head was held proudly, gamely, and Ruff had
to admire her.

Being passed from the hands of a butcher to those of a
murderer, she still had her dignity, her pride.

Hurly stirred in the rocks beside Ruff, and Ruff
turned with one motion, cocking and leveling his Colt.
Hurly's wide eyes stared into the muzzle of the revolver,
and his motion stopped abruptly.

Ruff returned his attention to the meeting. "Get
down, girlie," he heard Mix say, and she did so after
Stone Eyes had untied her hands. Mix shoved the girl
into the cabin and barred the door.

"Now," Stone Eyes said.

"Now you can see your rifles. You do have the gold,
don't you?"

Stone Eyes tossed a canvas sack to Mix, who examined
it briefly. Then he nodded to Clive and to Dawkins, who
sat aside, his eyes only on the two warriors who had ac-
companied the Ute chief.

Gorman Mix stuffed the gold into his coat pocket and
turned toward the mine, and Ruff felt his muscles
tighten. He glanced at Hurly, but the big man was as
rigid as before. Through the snow the six men walked,
three red, three white, none trusting any of the others.

"Lantern's out," Clive said dully.

"Goddam that brother of yours. He can't do a thing
right, can he?"

Stone Eyes did not like the feel of this. Perhaps fearing
a trap, he glanced at his men and nodded a warning.

"He took the mules out," Clive said suddenly, and
Ruff felt his heart quicken. The Colt was cold in his
hand.

As Clive held the lighted lantern up, Mix saw that it
was true. Ruff, just outside of the ring of light the lan-

tern cast, held utterly still. Through the drifting snow he could see a puzzled Mix glance around.

"What in hell was the dummy thinking?" Mix asked of no one in particular. He started to reach for his gun but saw Stone Eyes looking warily at him.

"I do not care to hear about mules," Stone Eyes said sharply. "Are the guns here or not?"

"Sure they are," Mix said, but there was an edge of uncertainty to his words now. Ruff saw Stone Eyes studying Mix carefully, mistrust obvious in his expression. "Let's have us a look-see."

"No. We will have look-see," Stone Eyes said. "You stay here."

Ruff smothered a bitter curse. That was not the way things were supposed to work. He prayed that Mix would argue, insist on going in with the Utes. But now Mix perhaps was not so sure the rifles were inside. He shrugged.

"All right."

Stone Eyes turned away and said across his shoulder, "Other eyes are on you, Gorman Mix."

"I figured," Mix replied with a shrug.

Stone Eyes entered the shaft, and Mix licked his lips nervously.

"Find 'em?" he called.

"Yes!" Stone Eyes called back. Mix relaxed visibly. Ruff heard the creaking of nails being pulled.

Stone Eyes called again from within. "They are—"

And then Ruff yelled, slapping the flank of the mule nearest him, and the rope tied around the upright timber at the mine entrance drew taut, stretching up out of the snow which had been hastily thrown over the line.

Ruff yelled again, Mix screamed a curse, and the timber gave way, the cave entrance creaking and then collapsing in a tumble of rubble and stone, sealing the Utes forever into the shaft with their beloved rifles.

Three shots were fired at Ruff, all blindly through the snow, which swirled and reduced visibility to inches. Ruff was already moving, following his predetermined plan of action. He didn't waste time firing back at Mix and Colter, but rushed toward the front of the cabin, the bodies of three mules between himself and their bullets.

He was to the door in seconds. It took another second to unbar the door, and he flung it open.

Lita Mancek stood stock still in the center of the room, her eyes wide. She didn't pause to ask time-wasting questions when Ruff curtly told her, "Let's go. They'll be here soon!"

She rushed from the room, and Justice roughly helped her into the saddle of one of the horses. He had the three mules and two other horses in tow on a long string he had devised while waiting for Stone Eyes to make his appearance.

Stone Eyes—he looked back toward the cave, where stone still rumbled down, bringing a shower of snow. Stone Eyes would have a little while to examine his rifles before he died. But there would be no joy in it. There was no one left to kill but his own men. Being the man he was, he might even do that if there was time before the air ran out on him.

Mix rushed around the corner of the house, and Ruff fired a round. The bullet whined off the stone cabin, nearly soundless above the shriek of the nightwind. But Ruff somehow saw clearly the groove it had cut in the old stone.

Mix fell trying to get behind the wall, and Ruff spurred his horse on, Lita riding beside him. From out of the wash of snow as they dipped down toward the river, an Indian's face appeared.

Weirdly painted, he screamed in anger and raised his old musket-rifle to his shoulder. Ruff touched off with his Colt and the man's face exploded in a mask of blood.

Lita felt her stomach turn over at the sight, but glancing at the tall man who rode beside her, she knew he had had no choice.

They splashed across the cold river and up into the timber, winding among the trees. Lita shouted to him, "We could go faster without towing all these horses, couldn't we?"

"We could," Ruff shouted back, "but they'd go a lot faster too if they caught their horses."

Ruff was leaving them afoot in the mountains, but he had no sympathy to spare for Mix. It was a matter of cold indifference to him whether the Utes or hard weather got Gorman Mix.

He was concerned only with his own safety and that of Lita Mancek. They had emerged again from the timber and now had to travel down the long, narrow canyon past Mix's guard.

"How will we get past him?" Lita asked when Ruff briefly told her how things were.

"I'm not sure we will," Ruff told her, "any more than I'm sure we can make it out of here without the Utes lifting our hair. But we'll try." He smiled, and as they rode she felt his hand reach out and close on hers. Somehow that was reassurance enough. There was strength in that hand, determination, and Lita felt more optimistic than she had for weeks. Despite the bleakness of the situation, the bitter cold, she smiled in return.

"When we come up on the guard," Ruff said, realizing that should be soon, for the man would not be posted far from the cabin, "I'll go ahead, assuming we see him first. I'll see what can be done. Maybe in this light he'll not recognize me right off. You'll have to hold back and see how it goes. If I go down, you'll have to go back as hard as it will be to do so, and try to find another way."

Things didn't work out that way. As they came

around a tight bend on the treacherous, rocky trail, they met the Dawkins kid nearly eyeball to eyeball.

He was riding slowly back toward the cabin, carrying a rifle in his hand. He jumped when he saw Justice and the girl, and his rifle came up.

"Who are you?" the kid asked, and it seemed absurd until Ruff recollected that the kid could never have seen them before.

Still, the kid was not stupid. How many pretty young women could there be riding these mountains? He peered intently at Lita.

"Friends," Ruff said calmly. "Just riding through. Headed for Leadville. It'll be warm there, kid, safe. No damned Utes, no chance of falling." He nodded toward the sheer drop beneath them, the cold water which raged past down the gorge. "There'll be whiskey, friends, a girl maybe," Ruff went on, measuring the Dawkins boy.

"Why the hell are you telling me all that?" he asked, his voice oddly high-pitched, perhaps with nervousness. The rifle he held trained on them trembled in his hands.

"Just reminding you of a few of the small things life has to offer." Ruff shrugged. "It's a bad night to end life. To be sprawled broken on the rocks, the life bled out of you, your eyes open to the snow."

"Dammit!" Dawkins shrieked. "I don't want to hear that."

"Just thought I'd make your choice clear to you, kid," Ruff said softly. "Because those are your options, you know."

"I've got the drop on you," he said uncertainly.

"Sure." Ruff nodded. "You'd get lead into me. But by God, kid, I'll get my Colt up and I'll get a shot off. I'll promise you that. And one shot is all I'll need. We might be spending a cold night together down there."

Lita heard the confidence in Justice's voice, saw the

uncertainty in the kid's eyes as they shifted to the deep, icy ravine below.

"My dad'll skin me," the kid said.

"You never saw us," Ruff replied evenly.

His rifle wavered, and for a moment Ruff thought he would squeeze that trigger. Then he nodded and repeated tonelessly, "I never saw you."

He lowered the hammer cautiously, his eyes on Ruff, and then he nudged his horse forward, squeezing between Ruff and the wall of stone which rose above them. The kid never looked back, and in a minute he was gone around the bend in the trail.

"Let's get lower," Ruff said.

Lita simply looked at him for a long moment, amazement in her eyes. Then she nodded.

"Let's do."

It was a slow five miles down out of the gorge. The weather had deteriorated to where Ruff could not see his horse's head half the time. They had to let the animals pick their own way down the treacherous path.

Once down, Ruff felt better about things despite the wall of snow which fell against them. It could be, of course, that young Dawkins had ridden directly to the cabin and Mix had taken his horse and set off in pursuit. But Ruff doubted that had been the kid's course of action. Dawkins had had enough of guns and hard weather.

Justice was more concerned about the Utes. He had no idea how many more there had been watching—unless that was Stone Eyes' bluff.

Would they pursue them, or would Stone Eyes' death deflate all of their ambitions and send them skulking back into their camp?

The storm worried him most.

It was actually warmer with the snow, but it was dry and very heavy, obscuring all vision, cutting away the rest of the world. The horses now moved through knee-deep drifts, and they were riding blind. In this weather they could simply ride off an escarpment or find themselves turned around, riding back toward the mountains.

"We have to stop somewhere," Ruff shouted, leaning close to Lita. With the wind raging, he had to repeat it, and she only nodded.

Ruff took hold of her reins now, not wanting to lose her, and she was content to have him do so. Ruff, finding his way by keeping the wind on his shoulder, made his way into the timber where he had camped two nights ago.

The trees embraced them, their bulk a shield against the cutting wind. It was dark and cold beneath the pines but far preferable to being on the snow-swept flats.

Following his own rule that a camp should always be on the highest ground possible, Ruff led Lita and the train of mules upward toward the ridge. They halted just below it where the wind was deflected by the stone and trees above them, but where they could see any pursuit below.

With luck—for on a night like this, the Utes would be deadly shadows moving through the snow and the pines.

Ruff took his Bowie and cut boughs from the pines to make a crude lean-to. It wasn't much, but it shielded Lita a little more, kept her a little drier.

When he had finished picketing the animals, Ruff crawled into the shelter beside her. She looked smaller than he had thought, huddled there, and a deal more beautiful with her hair swept back from her fine-boned face.

She trembled, and he handed her an extra blanket. "It smells of horse," he apologized, "but it's warm."

"Thank you." She took it timidly. This girl had been through a good deal; it would be a time before she was totally trusting.

"Thank you for all of it," she said, her face turned away. "I've never seen such brave acts."

"No? For my money your courage was a match for mine, Lita. It can't have been easy."

"No," she said looking shyly at him. "It wasn't easy. In fact, it was very difficult. But my father impressed on me very young that you must never give up, never throw hope away. After all, when hope is gone, there's very little left."

"A wise man, your father," Ruff said.

He sat with a blanket around his shoulders, his eyes alert to every shadow, each form. His Colt rested on his lap.

"Aren't you going to sleep?" Lita asked.

"No."

"Then I shan't either," she said. "It isn't fair." She was trembling again, and Ruff did not think it was with the cold. She had been wound up like a clock with tension and fear. Now, slowly, it was unwinding, and it was only now that the reaction to what had happened set in.

"Scared?" Ruff asked.

"No . . . yes," she admitted. "Very scared."

"Come here. I won't hurt you." He lifted his arm, and Lita scooted to him. He let his arm encircle her, and he held her tight through the long, bitter night.

13

MORNING BROUGHT BRIEF clearing. Ruff was up with the first gray light, preparing the horses for travel. The mules were sullen, wanting to eat, but there was nothing for them.

Lita had finally fallen asleep, and only as Ruff returned to the lean-to did she awaken. She peered out of the snow-covered shelter, her eyes dark and bright, her expression bemused. She looked at Ruff in daylight for the first time, uncertain if she liked what she saw, perhaps; maybe she had pictured him otherwise.

She stood stiffly and brushed the snow from her hair. With hands on hips she looked around and said with delight, "We've made it, then! It's actually over."

"Nearly." Ruff was a good deal more restrained in his optimism, surprising Lita.

"But can anything go wrong now?"

"Something can always go wrong, Lita."

The voice, somehow familiar, quite cold and menacing, came from behind them:

"Mr. Justice is a wise man, Lita. What he says is the truth. Something has gone quite wrong." Ruff recognized the voice now, and his hand drifted toward his holstered Colt.

"It is not necessary to die at this moment, Mr. Justice. Do not draw your weapon. Mine, as you see, is already in my hand. I am quite good with a handgun."

"I'll bet you are, Zardan," Ruff said, turning slowly to face the chief of the secret police.

"Zardan? Don't I know you? Yes," Lita said, "I've met you at my father's villa."

"You are correct, Lita Mancek," Zardan said with a bow. The smirk on his face was insufferable.

"You have this wrong, my dear Zardan," she said, stepping toward him. "Mr. Justice is my rescuer, not my abductor. I assure you—"

"I have nothing wrong," Zardan said sharply. He was dressed in a long fur coat, fur cap, and black leather gloves. He held a deadly-looking little revolver in his hand, the make unfamiliar to Ruff.

"The Baroness wants . . ." Ruff began.

Zardan's eyes flickered, and he interrupted with authority. He was a man used to others trembling before him, and he liked the power he had right now. He positively beamed with cruel self-assurance. "I am the only one here who is truly aware of what the Baroness Sophia wants," Zardan insisted.

"My sister knows I am here? She sent you?" Lita asked. Her voice wavered between hope and mistrust.

"But of course, Lita Mancek. As she sent Mr. Justice. As she hired Gorman Mix. Your sister is quite concerned over you."

There was a nasty little smile that went along with

that, and Ruff was beginning to get the picture. He let his hand drop closer to the butt of his Colt.

"I don't understand," Lita said, looking from Justice to Zardan. "We are all on the same side, are we not?"

Zardan laughed and said cruelly, "You are a child, living in a child's world, Lita Mancek."

"What do you mean?"

"He means your sister wants you dead," Ruff Justice said, his eyes fixed on Zardan's gun hand.

"You're joking!" Lita laughed, but the laugh was struck through with horror.

"Did I not say that Justice is a wise man?" Zardan asked her. "He has come to a slow understanding, haven't you, Justice?"

"I believe so. And I'm a damned fool for playing her game."

"Do not be bitter. The Baroness has fooled better men," Zardan said with what seemed a touch of wistfulness.

"What is this about?" Lita demanded. Her tiny fists were clenched, and she took a step toward Zardan.

"Power. Money," Zardan told her. "That is what it is usually about in this life, isn't it?

"You see," he explained, "your father is dying, Lita Mancek, and one of you must ascend the seat of power. Perhaps it means little to you, but I can assure you it means a great deal to the Baroness Sophia."

"Then let her have the power!" Lita said in frustration.

"Ah, if it were only so simple," Zardan replied. "But you and I know it is not. Your father has chosen you to succeed him—in the light of certain of your sister's past activities, he found your charming innocence preferable. Certain associates of mine opened your father's safe and read the will, so I know this is so."

"But don't you see," Lita burst out, "I don't care

about any of it! The intrigues, the affairs of state. I'd sooner stay in America. I'll sign papers—"

"To repudiate them later?" Zardan asked slyly. "No, you see, as long as you survive, Lita Mancek, you are a threat to your sister."

"Then why?" she asked wearily. "Why did you bother to send Mr. Justice? Why save me, give me hope and then destroy it?"

"To be sure," Zardan answered. "How were we to know you were dead? Gorman Mix is a sly man. He could very easily have claimed you were dead, accepted the reward, and later revealed that you were alive, hidden away in the mountains—it could have gone on endlessly, Lita Mancek."

"You needed her brought out, and I was fool enough to do it," Ruff said.

"Exactly. You were hired for that purpose. The Baroness wants to see her sister dead, to know it is her. Unfortunately, we did not find out until later that you were interested more in a cache of rifles than in performing your duties."

"And how did you find out?"

"A certain Captain Saranevo mentioned it in conversation. A man speaks voluminously when he believes his neck is about to be broken."

"But you snapped his neck anyway."

"It seemed prudent," Zardan said, as if Saranevo's life were of no more importance than that of a cockroach. "And although I am grateful to you, Mr. Justice—I am certain no one else could have done the amazing job you did in rescuing Lita—you too will have to die."

"And Lita?"

"Lita will return with me to Leadville. To meet her sister. For the last time."

The wind lifted the fur on Zardan's cap and coat. His dark eyes were obsidian, expressionless, hardly human.

He lifted his gun, and Ruff knew he was going to fire.

Only he didn't. There was a small sound as of a tree limb snapping, and Zardan lurched toward them. The front of his head was blown away, and blood showered the snow. He toppled forward, sprawled dead against the ground.

Ruff went to his knee, drawing his gun. The man appeared from behind a tree.

"You won't need that, Mr. Justice," Benny said. He turned Zardan over with his toe and then pocketed his own gun.

"Baroness." The little man with the big mustache bowed formally. "It is delightful to see you well."

"I don't know you." Lita said shakily. She kept her eyes deliberately averted from Zardan's gory corpse. "Or . . . do I?" She peered more closely at the cook. "Somehow . . ."

"I am one of those invisible men," Benny said with a smile which lifted his huge mustache slightly, "whom everyone sees and no one notices."

"My father's chef!"

"I am pleased you do remember," he said, bowing. "I have been your father's chef for twenty years. It has been an effective charade, covering my other duties quite neatly.

"For twenty years, that is to say, I have been one of your father's corps of personal bodyguards. With men like Zardan"—he nodded with distaste toward the corpse—"having infiltrated the secret police and the army, your father thought it advisable to form his own palace guard. Your father also suggested to the Baroness Sophia that it was wise to take her own chef with her on this tour of primitive America where the only available cooks might be savage Indians."

The snow had begun again, drifting through the pines, gently covering Zardan's body.

"I think perhaps now we should be returning," Benny said, glancing to the skies.

"Returning?"

"To Leadville, I mean," the cook said. "I am sure you still would wish to speak to your sister."

"What about the general, and Vice-Premier Chapek?" Ruff wanted to know.

"Innocent men, Mr. Justice. Brought along only for display, and, I suspect, to view the sad remains of Lita Mancek when they could be produced."

Lita shuddered, not liking to hear herself spoken of in that way. It was cold, and she turned to Ruff Justice. "I want to see her. I'm ready to ride."

"I'm ready too, Lita. I've a wish to see the Baroness Sophia Mancek myself."

Leadville was smothered in snow. Drifts five to six feet high lay along the windward side of the buildings along Union Avenue. The mines were shut down, for although underground it was no worse than it was during spring months, they simply could not be reached.

The saloons could be reached quite handily, it seemed, for only there did life in Leadville seem to be flourishing in the dead of winter; there and at the stately Ophir Hotel.

Lita had regained her vigor and her confidence. Dressed like a Ute squaw with an expensive European fur coat over her shoulders, she strode imperiously through the lobby of the Ophir, Ruff Justice and Benny beside her, causing heads to turn and the wary desk clerk to raise a silent hand in protest. His hand dropped once again at Ruff's cold glance, and they achieved the stairwell, marching to the second floor past a somewhat outraged matron.

At Benny's insistence they went first to the general's suite. He wore an embroidered silk dressing gown and a bewildered expression. He actually did lose his monocle this time as his eyebrows raised in startled amazement.

He kept muttering, "My dear, my dear," buzzing around the room searching for something he never found, until Ruff finally suggested that he dress.

Together the party progressed to the vice-premier's rooms. They sat then around an oval mahogany table, and Lita told the story from beginning to end, to the vice-premier's indignation and a chorus of "My dears!" from the general.

"So now what is there to be done?" Vice-Premier Chapek asked, looking from one face to the next, his palms turned upward.

"The Baroness Sophia must be arrested, obviously," Benny said.

"The scandal!" the general said, mopping his forehead.

But Chapek sternly told the military man, "This is hardly the time to be swayed by such considerations, General Ankirat."

The general muttered a vague disclaimer. Chapek turned to Ruff. "What about the American authorities?" he asked.

"There are some very serious charges to answer to," Ruff said, "but it might be very drawn-out and unsatisfactory. I doubt the American government will want to deal harshly with her. Probably nothing more than deportation. All in all, a waste of time."

"I agree," Benny said. The vice-premier glanced superciliously at the little man. One did not hold conferences with cooks. Benny, unperturbed, went on, "I am certain justice would be swifter, more equitable, at home, sir. His highness will certainly wish to have a voice in the deliberations."

"Baroness?"

"Perhaps," Lita said tonelessly, "after I have spoken to

my sister there will be no need to worry over such decisions."

There was a general silence in the room until Lita rose, folding her coat over the back of the chair, standing there in buckskins, her hair knotted back, looking capable and feral.

"If you will accompany me, Mr. Justice?"

"I'd be happy to," Ruff said with a smile.

The others followed without being asked as Lita opened the door and tramped down the hallway to Sophia's suite.

She knocked with authority on the door, and a hectic housemaid appeared.

"Madame is not receiving," she said.

"She's receiving," Lita said. She grasped the maid's shoulder and thrust her to one side, striding through the doorway with Justice, Benny, the general, and Chapek on her heels.

They burst into Sophia's bedroom, finding her propped up in bed, her hair exquisitely done, wearing a white satin bedrobe against the white satin of the bed.

Her eyes gave her away only momentarily, and then she recaptured her composure. She could have made a fine career of the stage, Ruff thought.

She made to rise. "Darling, Lita!" she exclaimed, her arms stretched out to embrace her long-lost sister.

"Darling Sophia," Lita replied purringly. Then she launched herself at Sophia headlong, and she landed on hands and knees on the bed, knocking Sophia back against the headboard.

"Lita!" Sophia screamed, and then fought back, but Lita was a wildcat. She yanked at Sophia's hair and ripped at her sister's dressing gown. Sophia ducked away, shoving at Lita, but her sister kept coming, slapping her face, her neck, clawing at her eyes.

"My dear, my dear!" Ankirat murmured. Chapek started forward, but Ruff put a hand on his shoulder.

"Let Lita have what's coming to her."

And Lita was having it. She tore her sister's dressing gown down the front, and Sophia's marvelous breasts bobbed free. The general squinted painfully; Chapek simply stared.

"You bitch!" Sophia squalled. She tried to cover her breasts, but that only gave Lita an opening to claw at her face, and so Sophia threw modesty to the winds and fought back, kicking and scratching.

Lita caught Sophia as she tried to make a run for it, and they toppled from the bed in a flash of legs, a tangle of arms.

They landed hard, and Sophia, on hands and knees, tears streaming from her eyes, tried to crawl away, but Lita caught the hem of her gown and yanked. It came off over Sophia's ankles, and she fell to her face, completely naked, as her sister, in buckskins, crawled up onto her back and sat pummeling her with tiny fists.

Sophia pounded a hand against the carpet. She sobbed uncontrollably, and finally Ruff walked to them, lifting Lita off the naked, beaten Sophia Mancek.

Lita kicked and wriggled in Ruff's arms, but he told her, "That's enough. You've given her plenty. You've won," and she slowly subsided.

Lita stood over her sister, her fists still clenched, her breast heaving, her face tight with slowly fading anger.

Benny had approached, and without expression he yanked a blanket from the bed and held it out to Sophia.

"Baroness."

She snatched the blanket from him without a word, her eyes bitterly fixed on Lita and Ruff Justice. Lita glared at her a minute longer, and then the tenseness drained from her, the anger, and she started crying herself, crying with relief, with anger, with frustration, and with bitterness against her sister and the fates.

She turned to Ruff and buried her face against his chest, and he stroked her back, watching as Sophia slowly rose and was escorted aside by the general and Benny.

Chapek stood immobile, watching it all, until Sophia was led away to dress, and then with a sharp exhalation he said, "Damnedest thing," and turned toward his own rooms.

14

THEY HAD JUST finished lighting the candles in the chandeliers, and the dining room was ablaze with light, warm with the murmur of conversation, when Ruff Justice entered the room.

She sat alone at a table near the wall, and Ruff crossed to her, smiling. Lita looked beautiful in green. The gown revealed her smooth shoulders and hinted at the lovely fullness of her breasts. She smiled as he took his seat. The candlelight caught the diamond pendant she wore and sparkled in her eyes.

Lovely she was—Sophia with the tightness, the telltale lines which revealed temper and cunning, smoothed and blurred by the bloom of health, the resiliency of youth.

"You look fine," he told her, and she blushed only slightly.

"And you, sir," she answered, examining his face by candlelight, the cool blue-gray eyes, the strong hands which emerged incongruously from the sharply tailored dark suit. "I'm not sure I don't like you better in buck-skins, however."

"I'm certain I prefer you in satin, Lita."

Their eyes met and held for a moment before the waiter, carrying a wine list and speaking with a terrible French accent, appeared beside the table.

"Monsieur?"

"Not for me," Ruff answered. Lita shook her head as well.

The waiter immediately produced menus, which they only glanced at. "It's been a while since I've had a steak," Ruff said. "Medium rare."

"The same," Lita chimed, simply to be rid of the waiter. When he was gone she faced Ruff, her chin on her hands. "I want you to come with me, you know. Just to visit if you can't stay. I'm not even sure I shall stay."

"I can't go," Justice told her

"Please?" Her hand rested on his. "I shall feel so much safer."

"With Benny you can feel secure, I think."

"But he is not so much fun. You have been to Europe, but have you skied? Our country is known for its slopes."

"I've never tried it. But this is just not the time, Lita. Really, it isn't."

"Father will want to meet you—he's doing surprisingly well, according to the latest letter. You could do worse, Justice," she said, leaning toward him. "We need a new chief of secret police. Or I'm sure you could have a commission in the army—choose your own rank."

"I don't think that would suit me, Lita."

"Then come as my guest!" she implored. "Stay a little time with us."

"I'd like nothing better," Ruff said. "But I can't now. Not just yet."

"But why not?"

"Mix."

Her brow furrowed. She looked at him intently, started to laugh, and then saw he was not joking in the least.

"Gorman Mix! You are still concerned with him?"

"I am. He's still alive. He's got a sackful of gold, and come spring he'll walk out of those mountains and live free and easy."

"Let the law handle it, Ruff!" she said, squeezing his hand.

"Handle what? Lita, they can't pin murder on him. No one saw it—not even I did. He killed my friend," he said, looking at those dark, liquid eyes of Lita Mancek intently. "And he has to pay for it."

"But you can't mean it!" She laughed. "You'd risk your life to go back up there? Why, the Utes probably have already killed them! Or they've starved."

"It could be. There's only one way to be sure," Justice said. "Gorman Mix and the Colters are killers. They killed Bryson Hargrove, and I know it. I know where they are. Now's the time, and I'm the man for the job."

"You're not!" Lita was momentarily infuriated. "You got out of those mountains only through sheer luck. You said as much yourself."

"That's right. Now I need a little more luck, because I'm going back after Gorman Mix."

She was silent. The waiter served their dinner, but neither of them touched it. "I'll be gone when you come back," Lita said finally, looking at her hands, which were folded in her lap. She glanced up and then quickly away, her hopes fading.

"I know you will."

"I have to go, you see!" She spoke rapidly, in some bewilderment. "My father is ill, there are matters of state, the problem of Sophia . . ."

"I know, Lita," Ruff said. He stretched out a hand to her, and after a long moment her hand reached out to meet his.

"But you'll come . . . sometime, I mean." Her eyes were glossy with barely suppressed tears. "I mean, you have been to Europe before, you said—with that Bill Cody show—so perhaps you'll come again."

"We'll put on a command performance," Justice told her. He squeezed her hand and then let it fall from his. "I promise you."

"Well, then . . ." Lita painted on a brave smile and straightened up, picking up her knife and fork. "That will be grand! We'll look forward to your visit."

She cut at her steak, still smiling. Then a single tear broke free, trickled across her cheek, and splashed against the table. Lita rose abruptly, nearly tipping over her chair, and as Justice watched, she rushed from the dining room, her napkin to her face.

"Waiter!" Ruff called the man with a gesture.

"Monsieur?" he asked.

"Clear it," Ruff said, waving his hand. The waiter frowned and observed the table, the untouched meals.

"It is over, the dinner, before it is started?" the little man asked.

"That's it in a nutshell," Ruff said. "Over before it's started." He rose, folded his napkin, and tossed a gold eagle onto the table to lie there and glitter coldly in the candlelight.

Justice walked up to his room. Entering, he stripped off his suit, gave himself that self-mocking glance in the mirror, and shook his head.

"You *are* insane," he whispered. "They're all right about that."

An aristocratic lady, a trip to Europe, a pleasant winter before the fire in her villa. And he had turned it down. Quite politely, firmly, turned Lita Mancek down.

Ruff pulled his longjohns from his bag and threw them on the bed.

As he stepped into them he felt reluctance growing. Yet he would return to the mountains, knew there was nothing this side of hell that could stop him.

It wasn't pride, it wasn't blood lust, which drove him, he knew. It was Bryson Hargrove lying cold in his grave.

What kind of man could enjoy any of it with the knowledge that he had done nothing to bring Bryson's killers to justice? No matter how beautiful the woman, no matter how tempting the offer.

He knew there were men of that kind, and plenty of them. He also knew that Ruff Justice was not one of them. And so he dressed, pulling his buckskins on, strapping on his gunbelt.

There was a tap at the door, and Ruff opened it. Benny stood there, wearing a fur coat.

"I saw Lita Mancek. She said you were going back."

"That's right," Justice told him.

"I will go with you then. I can be helpful at times," he said with a smile.

"No, Benny. It's my job to do. Lita needs you."

"She has the soldiers." He shrugged. "The general, and Chapek. She does not need me."

Ruff studied the man carefully, recognizing a brave, solid man. He wagged his head and said, "No, Benny. I appreciate the offer, I really do. But this is my country, my debt. You've got your own obligations at home, beside Lita. I'd feel better about everything if I knew you would be right behind her."

"All right." Benny shrugged again. "I have offered and you have refused. Perhaps you are right, Justice. You may rest assured that I shall be at hand if Lita needs anything. I hope that will make it easier for you to go."

"It will." Ruff smiled and thrust out his hand, and Benny took it, grinning beneath his wildly flaring mustache.

When Benny was gone he finished dressing, moving methodically, not thinking about Lita or anything superfluous to the task at hand.

The bay and the pack horse, had come back to the stable. The gray which Ram had given him had not. Possibly it had gone back to its old habitat, the Ute camp, now deserted.

All right then, he needed a good saddlehorse. A strong, heavy animal to fight through those drifts, preferably mountain-bred, but certainly no mustang pony. That and a new rope.

He had no intention of trying that ice slide again, but then there is more than one use for a rope.

Ruff walked out of his room, carrying his small satchel. He closed the door behind him, started to turn toward Lita's room, hesitated, and, pivoting sharply on his heel, strode to the staircase and went down to the desk.

He settled his bill, left the stachel in storage, and went out into the windless, frozen evening. At the stable he found a sturdy, deep-chested ox of a bay to ride, and as he was settling up with the hostler the shadow fell across the earth at his feet.

He turned slowly, letting his hand fall to his gun butt. The Dawkins kid stood there, his eyes narrowed.

"Hello, Mr. Justice," the kid said.

"Hello. You got out, did you?"

"I got out. Looks like you're going back."

"Does it?" Ruff handed the hostler his money and turned to face the kid. The stableman drifted rapidly to one side. "Was there something else, Dawkins?" Ruff asked.

"Yeah. I followed you over here, Justice. To say thanks. I guess we both know I might never have seen this day."

"Make sure you live it so you see tomorrow," Ruff advised him.

"I intend to."

Justice swung into leather. The kid stepped aside, and Ruff rode past him, trailing the bay. He rode out into the still, blue night and looked to the far mountains where a white quarter-moon bleached the ragged peaks.

He tugged his hat low and heeled the bay forward, leaving his tracks in the slushy main street of Leadville, Colorado.

He camped on a low hillrise studded with cedar and spruce that evening, chancing a fire—Mix would never see it. He was snowbound in that deep gorge. There had been a brief melt and then a hard freeze, and the trees surrounding Ruff were glazed with ice.

Balls of ice—snow which had melted and then refrozen—hung on the trees, glittering like crystal in the light of the silver moon.

The firelight caught the ice, and the ice jewels glittered with reddish light. It was beautiful, magical. He sat on a skinned log, watching the flats, silvery, smoothly undulating, and the distant, somber peaks.

He chewed on salty jerky and salty biscuits, washing it down with coffee. He thought ruefully of the steak he had not eaten that evening. But he had had no appetite then.

He rolled up next to the log to sleep. There the fire had melted the snow, and the log itself acted as a reflector for the fire's warmth.

Morning dawned cold, beautiful. Ruff rose from his bed stiffly, stamping his feet to hurry the circulation, starting the fire, which he stood near for longer than he should have.

The coffee, scalding hot when he poured it, was tepid in minutes. Sunset bled across the vast snowfields, pinkening them, highlighting the glassy pines with gold.

He had to rub the ice from the horses' backs with a saddle blanket. They looked at him morosely, accusingly.

The mountain-bred horse had been able to paw the snow away and find some dead grass to forage on. The pack animal was not so clever, and Ruff had to clear a patch of graze for it.

He packed his roll as the horses fed on the poor grass, and then, with the sun peering over the deep-blue forest to the east, he trekked out, steam rising from the horses' nostrils and their flanks as they traced deep tracks across the virgin snow.

The purple mountains capped with snow seemed no nearer at nooning when Justice stopped briefly to rest the horses and to feed himself with his own poor fare. More jerky, a can of peaches opened with his Bowie, and more dry biscuits.

Within an hour they were moving again, and now the snow was to the horses' bellies. They moved forward in jackrabbit motions, bucking through the heavy snow for most of an hour before they reached the timbered foothills where the land rose and the snow was shallow.

They circled the line of hills, sticking to the timber. The ground was slushy underfoot; the scent of pine was heavy, nearly overpowering in the air. A pair of complaining crows winged across the deep-blue sky, casting darting shadows against the bluish snow.

Once Justice passed a foraging grizzly, and he steered wide of the big silvertip. If that bear was up and prowling, it could only be because of ravening hunger. Once in Wyoming he had a packhorse pulled down by the haunches by a silvertip no larger than this one, and he wanted none of this bear's trouble.

In late afternoon he reached the mouth of Dead Cow.

Justice drew up slowly, and with a slow, heavy curse he surveyed the entrance to the canyon. It was worse than he had expected.

The snow lay in forty-foot drifts along the rocky gorge. There must have been a slide; they had seen a lot of snow lately, but not that much.

What now? He lifted his eyes to the far peaks. They looked treacherous, impossible under these conditions. The only satisfaction he got out of the sight was the certain knowledge that Gorman Mix had not gotten out of there alive.

The river roared past, tunneling under the massive drifts, forming arches and hollows in its passage. He wondered. . . .

How swift was that current? How deep the river? It was a treacherous, thundering river, but perhaps it could be followed for a little ways, far enough to clear the avalanche.

He rode toward it, looking with lowering optimism at the raging whitewater which tore its way through the ice and snow, at the slick, treacherous gray rock lining the riverbed.

The river was a good five feet deep at that point and running with the speed and strength of a locomotive. Yet upriver a quarter of a mile, he thought he could see where the avalanche had tailed off. There it might be possible to achieve the broken trail up to the Stanford Mine.

Possible. With the big horse, maybe. He patted the horse's neck, reassuring it. He looked at his pack animal, knowing it would have no chance.

It was time for a decision, and there were only two

options—try to buck the raging river's current, risking being swept away, drowned, and deposited in some distant lake, or turning back.

For the second time in that week, Justice cut the packhorse loose to make its way back to Leadville. It should know the way by now, he thought wryly.

Still stroking the big horse's neck, he said, "Think you've got it in you?" The horse's ears pricked up, and it shied as it eyed the torrential river, perhaps having some animal awareness of this man's mad scheme.

"Let's have at it," Ruff said, taking a deep breath. The roar of the river was in his ears. The snow loomed overhead in a suspended fall, awaiting only the slightest whim of gravity to crush Justice and that big horse.

Ruff eased the bay into the creek. The horse fought the reins, then surrendered to the will of its master. The water was swift, clotted with ice, knee-deep on the horse, and Ruff could feel it struggling against the current, its hoofs sliding on the slick stone beneath it.

Gently he turned the horse upstream, his own breath coming in tight gasps. "Easy," he told the horse. "Easy, now." He didn't want to make speed, he only wanted to make it, and the horse waded ahead.

A spectacular bridge of snow and ice arched over the river, rising some fifty feet into the sunlight. The horse was to its belly, and Ruff felt the current twist and nudge the bay, threatening to sweep its feet from under him.

"Just a little farther," Ruff said, trying to encourage the animal. If the horse panicked he was a dead man. White water roared past, slamming against the huge gray stones along the bottom, sending spumes of cold spray high into the air.

He glanced up at the blue ice of the majestic arch overhead and walked the horse slowly forward, letting the wary animal pick its own footing no matter how long it took to take each step. The current seemed even quicker now, and the water was to the stirrups, but Ruff could see the end of the tunnel, see a small alcove where they could step from the river . . . if they made it that far.

It was a slow, intense five minutes before they were free and the game horse scrambled up onto the bank, shuddering.

Ruff turned to glance back down the river. Then he shook his head in amazement at the things a man will try. He patted the horse's neck and scratched its head between the ears. His eyes lifted to the high trail. He was not far from where he had met the Dawkins kid, he thought, but he saw no easy way up.

The gorge itself dead-ended not half a mile farther, so if he was to find a way to the rim trail it had to be soon.

When he found it it was not a trail, but another slide. Snow had rushed down a narrow canyon, carrying earth and stone, breaking the trail away. But it was just what Ruff needed.

Turning the horse, he clambered up over the deep snow and jumble of concealed rock. The path stretched up and down the canyon, and Ruff was beside it now, but he urged the horse on, wanting to climb above the gorge.

Finally, breathless, they reached the summit of the hill. Dead Cow Gorge was gouged out of the snowy earth below them. The river rushed past. Beyond that the flats spread for miles, and there were only indistinct patches of gray-green far beyond to indicate the vast forests.

Yet Justice looked backward for only a minute. He was interested in what lay ahead.

To the west the broken trail wound up the gorge to the old mine. Beyond that the Rockies spread in untamed grandeur. He spared only a moment's glance for the high mountains and then let his eyes return to the abandoned Stanford mine. For there, quite distinct in the clear air, smoke rose from the old stone cabin.

15

IT WAS COMING to darkness in the high country, the shadows bleeding out from the canyons, creeping from beneath the trees to reclaim the land. Logic advised Ruff Justice to wait for morning light, but there was no patience in the man on this evening.

A killing time had come, and there was anger prodding him onward.

He wove his way carefully across the rocks, through the scattered, wind-torn pines, until he was overlooking the Stanford, which lay deep in snow half a mile beneath him. He looked once at the old mine shaft, noting without pride or anger, shame or pleasure, that Stone Eyes still lay entombed there with his war guns.

The shadows were deep in the valley, and the smoke still rose from the old stone chimney. Gorman Mix was readying his evening meal—it would be the last meal of his life.

Justice led his horse away from the rim and settled in to wait for full dark. As he waited he checked his guns—the rifle had picked up water in the river. Then, tilting back against the rough, cold bark of a massive ancient pine, he rested briefly, opening an eye now and then to watch the downward progress of the sun, the slowly settling mantle of darkness.

The clouds blotted out the stars and the land was dark when Ruff rose. He walked to the edge of the broken hill and squatted, watching the cabin, his rifle across his knees.

There was a light in the window, smoke rising steadily from the chimney. The snow was drifted up against the cabin nearly to the eaves on three sides. The front had been cleared somewhat.

Ruff rose, inhaled deeply, slowly, and slipped down into the valley. The night was cold and would soon grow colder for some of them.

He made the sparse stand of timber behind and beyond the house and sat there for most of an hour, watching. No one came and no one went. Gorman Mix seemed to have no guard posted. If there was a man out there, he had no sensitivity to cold. The night was bitter. Now and then an ice-laden branch cracked off a tree with a sound as loud as the report of a gun.

Ruff waited a time longer and then quickly, on cat feet, made his way to the back of the house. There was a thick crust of ice on the snow piled around the house, and he walked up onto the drift, careful to test his weight first.

He made it to the roof, took careful hold, and swung up. There was ice on the old shingle roof, and as he took his first tentative step, the roof creaked.

Ruff held his position, but no one emerged from the cabin. More cautiously he inched up the inclined roof until he was to the chimney.

Smoke billowed up—they were using damp wood now, obviously—and sparks stung his eyes. Justice slipped out of his sheepskin, balled the coat up, and jammed it into the chimney.

Shivering in shirtsleeves, he moved to the front of the roof and waited, crouched against the ancient gray shingles.

He didn't have long to wait. Within five minutes he heard the door open, saw a patch of light fall against the snow, and a coughing man stepped out. It was Hurly, and he must have caught Ruff's silhouette against the night sky, because he slapped for his sidearm even as Clive, also choking, stepped out of the cabin.

Ruff saw Hurly's gun come up from behind his sights. Justice touched off, and Hurly was tagged. He spun around, clutching at his good arm, a yowl of pain filling the night.

Justice immediately switched his sights to Clive. Clive Colter already had his gun in his hand, already was firing, and Justice winged a shot back, drawing back from the edge of the roof for protection.

"It's Justice!" he heard Clive bellow. And then Ruff felt his foot slip. He cursed the ice and tried to steady himself, but the foot kept going.

The problem was more than ice. His boot had gone right through the old, dilapidated roof, and his leg followed. Ruff grabbed at the roof, but it only fell away in a larger section. He heard his rifle clatter away down the roof, saw the blade of flame from another shot crease the sky, and then he crashed through the roof, thudding against the floor beneath him practically at Gorman Mix's feet.

The breath was driven out of Ruff as he landed flat on his back. He was seeing stars, but he was alert enough to see the cruel face of Gorman Mix above him and then to watch as Mix kicked out viciously with a boot, jerking Ruff's head around, putting out all the lights.

*   *   *

It was cold. His hands were not working. Slowly Ruff's eyes opened, and he discovered the reasons. There was a gaping hole in the roof of the old stone cabin, and although a low fire was burning, the wind, carrying light flakes of new snow, whipped through the hole, chilling it. His hands were strapped behind him.

He was sitting in an old wooden chair, tied at the ankles and wrists. As his head came up he saw Gorman Mix watching him from a slovenly bunk. Mix had a shotgun in his hands, and he came to his feet as Ruff's eyes opened.

Clive was bent over a man on the other bunk, and looking beneath Clive's arm he could see Hurly, his face ashen, his shirt painted with blood. Ruff wondered how Hurly would look wearing two slings, as he would have to now.

"Glad you could drop in," Mix said. Ruff didn't have time to respond before Mix's big fist shot out and slammed into his ear, setting off bells. Ruff felt blood dripping from his ear and had a moment to reflect on that before Mix's fist slugged him again, toppling him from the chair.

Clive looked around greedily.

"He's mine, he's mine—you said so," the big man said. He had that deadly truncheon in his hand. This time he would finish what he had begun on the train. Ruff cringed mentally at the memory of that beating.

His mind scrabbled for an idea, anything to keep Clive Colter off him. "If you kill me you haven't got a chance," Ruff said.

"Go to hell," Clive said, lifting the club. Ruff closed his eyes, expecting the blow, but after a second nothing had happened. He peered up at Mix, seeing that he had got hold of Clive's wrist.

"What do you mean, Justice?" Mix wanted to know. He crouched down, pulling Ruff's head up by the hair.

"He don't mean nothin'," Clive cried. "Let me have 'im!"

"Shut up, Clive." Mix slammed Ruff's head back against the floor and stood, rubbing his chin.

"I'm warning you, Mix," Ruff said. Mix roared with laughter.

"You're warning me!"

"That's right," Ruff told him coolly. "If you kill me you'll hang."

"What happened to you, Justice?" Hurly asked, taking his ear and twisting it until it felt as if he would twist it off. "That fall knock your brains loose?"

"You think I came up here alone, you damned fool?" Ruff exploded.

Mix's face went slack for a moment. He glanced at Clive. Hurly moaned in the corner.

"Why would he?" Mix asked himself or Clive, who stood there dumbly, truncheon ready.

"No one would, you fool," Ruff said.

"Where are they then?" Clive jeered.

"Sit me up. I can't talk down here."

"Go to hell. Talk there and like it."

"They're behind me. Six men," Ruff lied. "If you kill me you'll swing."

"We'll hang anyway."

"Not for running guns, you won't," Ruff argued. "Ten years at the most. There's no proof you killed the colonel. No one saw it, not even me."

Gorman Mix was thoughtful. "Get outside, Clive."

"It's snowin'!" Clive protested.

"Get outside and find some cover. Keep your eyes open."

Hesitantly the big man turned toward the door.

"Wait a minute, Clive," Mix said. He had a new idea. "If there's others, why are you here alone?" he asked Ruff.

"I came ahead."

"Why?"

"I wanted to kill you," Ruff said. "I know they can't hang you for what you did to Hargrove. I meant to do you myself."

"Get outside, Clive," Mix said. His dark face was thoughtful. What Justice said was logical enough. Why *would* he come alone? "Get yourself into that chair," he told Ruff.

"How?" Ruff asked.

"Don't then—I don't give a damn," Gorman Mix said. He returned to the bunk, where he sat meditatively. He watched as Ruff managed to sit up on the floor, back to the wall, and rise against it. Then Justice hopped to the chair, where he sat, throwing his head back.

Mix was thinking ahead now too. He had to figure there was a posse out there. In that case, he at least had Justice as a hostage . . . if there was a posse. Justice was sly enough to make the whole thing up.

"If they don't come, I'm killing you," Mix said.

"Hell, Mix, I know that," Justice said. He tried the ropes, but they were tightly knotted. His mind worked feverishly. He had run his bluff, but it was a bare bluff—when that imaginary posse didn't show Mix would simply shoot him and dump him into the snow to wait for spring thaw.

"How far ahead are you?" Mix wanted to know.

"They wanted to come in at daybreak. I couldn't wait," Ruff said convincingly.

"You'll wait now," Mix said. "Until dawn. If no one shows, you die. If they do, well, I'll see what I can work out."

That was all there was to do, Mix decided. He couldn't risk killing Justice just now—there was a chance the man was telling the truth. And if there was a posse out there, it was best to wait and try to bluff their way out of it with Justice as hostage. Mix wasn't fool enough to think he, Clive, and an injured Hurly could walk out of this winter camp.

"We'll just wait," Mix said, leaning back against the wall. He had the hammers on that ten-gauge drawn back and his finger on the triggers.

It was going to be a long night and a brief morning.

There was no lull in Gorman Mix's vigilance. He seemed to take some sort of perverse pleasure in sitting there, just watching. Ruff was growing desperate. There was no posse, would be no help, and he knew it. A hundred wild plans flitted through his brain, but he had to cast each one aside.

He waited for some break, some opportunity, but none offered itself. Mix got up three times to feed fresh wood into the fire, but he moved cautiously, keeping his distance from Ruff, and it was absurd anyway to think of lurching from that chair, bound hand and foot, to attack an armed man.

He worked on the ropes, but it was useless. The knots were good ones. Twice Clive came in, complaining about the cold, and twice Mix sent him back out.

Now and then Hurly moaned. He was feverish now and thrashed about on the bunk. Mix nodded at Hurly.

"Clive wants to kill you for doin' that to his brother, and I reckon he will."

Ruff had the same morbid conviction. Beaten to death by Clive Colter in the high-up mountains. It was an odd place to end it, yet the way he had lived, rushing toward disaster, it was a wonder he had made it this long.

The door slammed open again. It was Clive, and he pleaded, "God almighty, Gorman! It's thirty below out! I can't take no more."

With a sigh Mix swung his feet to the floor.

"I'll spell you." He glanced at the sky through the roof, and with a start Ruff realized that it was gray, growing light. "I don't expect I'll have to stand too long. You keep your eyes on him, Clive, or I'll have your skin."

"I'll watch him, all right," Clive promised. His eyes gleamed maliciously. Mix leveled a warning finger.

"Don't you start beating on him. Not just yet."

"I could just soften him up a little," Clive insisted.

"Just watch him!" Mix thundered. Then he went out, pulling the door shut behind him, closing out the icy wind which gusted down the gorge.

Clive checked his brother, finding Hurly's fever worse, and then settled malignantly, staring at Ruff, his truncheon always ready.

Ruff was growing desperate now. The sky was definitely light and his hopes were narrowing rapidly. He looked around the room, trying to find some means of escape.

The fire burned low in the hearth, hot in Clive's dark eyes. Hurly was burning up in the flames of a fever. Clive thudded that deadly truncheon against the side of the bunk slowly, rhythmically. His rifle was propped up beside him, twelve feet from Ruff's chair, where he sat strapped wrists and ankles. Hurly had a gun, but it was in his holster . . . why was he thinking about guns? Dammit, could he cross the room, pick up a gun, fire it from behind his back? The sky through the gaping hole in the roof grew pale.

"Soon," Clive muttered.

"The posse will be here soon," Ruff warned him. "You'd be better off packing instead of wasting your time staring at me."

"Soon," Clive repeated, slapping the truncheon against the frame of the bunk. "That's a terrible thing you done to Hurly, Mr. Justice. He ain't been the same man for a long while."

"Then I've done him some good."

"You shut up!" he shouted, rising with his eyes flashing.

"Sit down—you know Mix doesn't want you beating on me."

Clive took a step nearer. "What's he gonna do—fire me?" He chuckled mirthlessly. The notion had settled into his dull mind; there was nothing at all Mix could do. "I'll leave you alive," Clive Colter said.

Justice kicked out with his feet, but Clive laughed, knocking his legs aside. Justice toppled from the chair, and Clive moved in.

The distant shot rang out, and they heard it ricochet off the stone wall of the house. Hurly paused in midstroke, his head twisting toward the door. A second shot was fired at the house.

Benny, Ruff thought. "It's the posse," he told Clive.

Clive kicked Ruff in the chest, snatched up his rifle, and bolted for the door, his heavy feet shaking the planks.

Ruff didn't hesitate a moment. His chest was shot through with pain, but this was his only chance, and he knew it. He wriggled like a maddened caterpillar to the door, kicked it shut, and got to his knees. With his teeth he drew the latch string in.

Three shots were fired from outside, one from some distance, two from close beside the house. Hopping madly to the fireplace, Ruff saw Hurly Colter's fever-glazed eyes on him. The big man's face drew taut with pain as he tried to reach his gun with his shattered, bloody arm.

Ruff flung himself to the floor, scooting his back nearer to the fire. Hurly had gotten hold of his pistol, but as he tried shakily to level it at Ruff, it slipped from his useless hand and clattered to the floor.

How much time was there before they broke the door

down? There was no telling. Ruff heard another volley of shots from outside.

Twisting around, he thrust his hands into the fire. Pain shot through his hands, terrible, shocking pain, as he tried to burn through the ropes with a hotly glowing ember.

The flame singed Ruff's hair, and the ember ate at his raw flesh. He could smell meat burning, rope burning, and then he was free.

He rolled from the fireplace, not wanting to look at his hands. A shoulder was thrown against the door once, twice, and Ruff saw the ancient planking buckle and collapse as Clive Colter, like a roaring bull, broke through into the cabin.

Ruff dove to one side, fumbling for the pistol Hurly had dropped. He came around with it, firing as Clive touched off a rifle shot. Clive's bullet thudded into the floor beside Ruff's bound legs, but Ruff's shot was better.

His bullet took Clive Colter at the base of the throat and drove the big man back against the wall. He was already dead as he slumped to the floor, blood streaming from his wound.

Ruff hurriedly untied his ankles, his eyes flickering from the doorway to Hurly Colter, who was staring at the huge crumpled form of his brother, his eyes awash with tears, his big mouth drawn down in anguish.

Ruff was free and to his feet. He inched toward the door, his heart racing. The cold wind met him as he dove outside, rolled to his feet, and drew back the hammer on his Colt.

Nothing. Mix was gone. He was alone in the cold, wind-swept yard.

And then he saw him. A flash of color against the snow. Gorman Mix was making for the forest, running, stumbling through the knee-deep snow.

Mix halted, winged a wide shot at Ruff, and kept on,

arms and legs churning wildly as he fought his way toward the perimeter of the pine woods.

Ruff stood there a minute, a tall, battered man in the snow. His hands were scorched by fire, his long hair wild, singed. The fire still burned in his blistered hands and in his heart. The Colt in his hand was ice-cold. He started slowly forward, jog-trotting after the man hiding in the forest.

16

A SHOT FROM the snow-clad forest sang overhead, and Ruff swerved, dipping into a hollow. But he never stopped; he did not fire back. He simply trotted on, the cold wind in his face.

There had been no shots from the opposite hillside. If Benny was up there—it had to have been Benny—then likely he was dead.

Mix fired again, from a new position. He was still moving, running eastward now, and with sudden apprehension Ruff thought of the horse he had left tethered on the rim of the broken hill. If Mix got to the horse he would be long gone, leaving Ruff to face the long winter with only the corpses of the Colter brothers for company.

Justice quickened his pace, wanting to make the woods himself. In the flats he was a sitting duck, and Mix would not miss every time.

He made his rush toward the trees, flattened out as a

bullet whined overhead, and rolled behind a jumble of snow-glazed boulders.

Justice did not stay down. He rolled to the far side and dashed forward, the woods a bare fifty yards away. Mix's rifle boomed again, and Ruff felt the searing pain flare up in his shoulder. He went down in a heap, spun around by the force of the .44-40 slug. Blood seeped from his left shoulder.

He forced himself to rise, to run on through the blur of pain. Lying against the snow he would have been a dead target for Mix.

Another bullet, low and left, dug a furrow of snow near Ruff's feet, and then he was into the dark comfort of the woods. Throwing back his head, he gasped for breath, leaning heavily against the damp, dark trunk of a pine tree.

Angrily he tore his scarf off and wrapped his arm, hardly stemming the flow of blood at all. Then he stumbled on, weaving through the trees.

There was no shot from Mix for three long minutes. Ruff dipped into a hollow and clambered up the far side, the icy pine needles slick underfoot.

He rose out of the hollow, and the gun rang out, tearing a chunk of bark from the pine beside him, revealing the white meat of the tree. Ruff went to a knee and fired at the darting figure of Gorman Mix, but Mix was behind the trees again and the shot whined harmlessly off into the forest.

Ruff staggered on, his breath coming raggedly. He caught a glimpse of Mix, but before he could bring his pistol up the man was gone again, vanished behind the trees.

Looking up through the veil of hair, the sweat, Ruff saw with growing anxiety that Mix was circling toward the broken hill, toward the horse, and he urged himself on.

But his legs were rubbery. He was dizzy with the loss of blood, and now, as the trees thinned, the snow was deeper.

Ruff fell to his knees. The snow was to his waist as he knelt there, panting like a dog on a summer day. Blood trickled down his sleeve and stained his hand, dotting the new snow with flecks of crimson.

He forced himself to rise, forced himself to run on. Mix fired from the hill, but Ruff didn't even slow or try to veer away. He simply ran, the Colt as heavy as an anvil in his hand.

Plodding through the snow, he made the base of the hill. It rose here sharply, snow-mortared blocks of gray granite. He stood there, his arms dangling, looking upward.

It was sheer stone for a hundred feet. Mix had clambered up, using the weather-formed splits for handholds. But with a game arm, Ruff doubted he could make it without falling.

"You can't turn back, Mr. Justice," he told himself wearily. Then, tucking his pistol snugly behind his waistband, he had at it.

Where ice had settled between the rocks it had frozen and wedged them apart. Ruff thrust his good hand into the lowest of these and clawed his way upward, his pulse hammering in his head.

His right arm had to carry the burden. The left was nearly useless. He had a good twenty feet to go when he slipped and grabbed desperately with his left hand to save himself. His body coursed with pain at that maneuver, and he clung to the rocks, his face streaming perspiration, as the ugly shock of pain slowly ebbed.

He had a black image form in his mind as he hung there—he could see Mix's dark, savage face. See the man waiting at the rim above with his gun in hand, ready to blow Justice's head off his shoulders. He could almost see himself falling backward into the cold snow far below. . . .

He climbed on. There was no way he could keep his pistol ready. Finally, apprehensively he found the rim of the hill and pulled himself up and over, rolling onto the flat ground.

Mix was not there. Ruff looked around in wonder, got unsteadily to his feet, and plodded on, gun in his hand once again.

Where was the horse? He could not even recall—it seemed like weeks since he had left the bay. Mix's bootprints were distinct in the snow, and Ruff ran on, following the outlaw across the broken ground, through the sparse timber.

He fell suddenly, without warning. His legs had simply given out, and he sat there angrily, rubbing his thighs, trying to get them to respond to his mind's urging.

He saw the shadow beyond the small stand of broken cedars, and he blinked, wiping his eyes. The horse—he had seen the horse, or so he thought. But it was not the right horse, and now as he looked again, it was gone.

His mind was playing tricks on him. He thought for a moment that it was the gray which Ram had given him and which he had lost. But it could not be. That horse was either fifty miles away or dead from cold and starvation.

Ruff shook his head, glanced once again toward the cedars, and trudged on.

Mix appeared suddenly from behind the boulders, and Ruff saw his gun erupt with flame, felt the bullet *whiff* past his ear. Justice fired back, the Colt bucking twice in his hand.

His shots missed. He saw chips of rock fly from the stone where his bullets had impacted. But Mix howled with pain.

Either a ricochet or flying splinters of stone had hit Mix in the face, and as Ruff watched, Mix tried to stem the flow of blood. It leaked through his fingers, and the outlaw pawed at his eyes, trying to clear his vision.

Ruff clambered over the rocks, circling, and Mix fired angrily. Three, four, five shots ricocheting off the rocks. But Justice went on, circling, moving in a crouch, and then he suddenly was above Mix, standing on a snow-frosted yellow boulder not ten feet from the badly bleeding outlaw.

The wind rushed past Justice, a cold wind. A dying wind.

"Mix," he said softly.

The outlaw spun, his bellow echoing across the hillside as he brought his Winchester to his shoulder, the blood gushing from his feral face.

Mix fired, but it was too late. Justice had calmly leveled his Colt, taking the time to sight and he squeezed off. His bullet slammed into Mix's chest, driving the outlaw back against the boulder behind him, and Mix's shot went high and wild.

Ruff cocked the Colt again and coolly fired again. Mix's body jerked convulsively, and he slid to the snow. Ruff fired once more and then again, but the hammer fell on an empty round, and there was nothing to do but to stand on that wind-swept rock, watching the life seep out of Gorman Mix, watching the far, empty mountains.

The wind suddenly felt very cold, and Justice felt his legs going again. He fell hard and landed on his arm, raw pain surging through him.

The skies had grown dark, and it was going to snow again—a hard, bitter snow.

Ruff rolled over and got to hands and knees. His arms would barely support him. He had to get down off of that hill. If he could make it back to the cabin somehow . . .

But his eyes grew blurry. The world flipped over, turned to water, was flooded with colors. Ruff opened his eyes and found that it had grown darker yet. Snow drifted down, and he saw that his chest was covered with an inch or more of the stuff.

He wriggled his arm, rolled over heavily, and crawled forward. His left arm was stiff, filled with angry pain, and he collapsed, face down in the snow.

Thunder boomed up the long canyon, shaking him to his senses. He tried to rise again, could not, and fell back.

He was going to die on that mountain—he knew that now. He would die and be covered with snow, and when it thawed someone would find the skeletons of four men up here and wonder what had gone before.

Ruff lifted his head at the sound of footsteps. Someone crunched across the fresh snow toward him. Who? He peered through the flurry of snow at the shadowy figure, and he whispered:

"Benny?"

But even as he spoke he knew it was not Benny. The cook was long gone, riding the rails across the nation, preparing to sail back across the sea to his own country.

She got down beside him on her knees, and the blanket she threw over him was warm, as warm as her body when she leaned near and whispered.

"I told you I would not go with my father. I told you I wanted a man to winter with. You, Ruff Justice," Yarna said. "Those men wanted to hurt you and spoil my winter, and so I shot at them. And now it is done."

She helped Ruff to a sitting position and gradually got him to his feet. She helped him back toward the gray horse.

Yarna stood beside him, studying the gray, rolling clouds. Her dark hair drifted across her pretty face, and she smiled, nodding with satisfaction.

"This storm will last a very long time, Ruff Justice.

You can go nowhere now, and I think your war is done, is it not?"

He nodded, and she smiled again. Taking the reins to Ram's gray war pony, she led the way back toward the old stone cabin.

WESTWARD HO!

The following is the opening section from the
next novel in the gun-blazing, action-packed new
Ruff Justice series from Signet:

RUFF JUSTICE #4: WIDOW CREEK

1

THE RIVER WAS a quiet, rambling thing. Black and murmuring beneath starlit skies. The massive oaks along the banks nodded in the silent night breeze as the great paddle-wheeler churned upriver.

Ruff Justice stood at the stern rail, watching the night and the river, which seemed to be made of black silk. The steamboat's paddles stirred up brief, angry ripples of white water, but the night smoothed them over, darkening the waters again.

Not a trace was left of the steamboat's passing. No more trace than a man leaves in his rapid passage across this earth, Justice thought. He turned with a sigh, leaning his back against the rail, listening to the night sounds—the grumbling of frogs along the riverbank, the splashing of the paddle wheels, the vague whispering of the night wind.

He was a tall man, his hair worn long, flowing across his shoulders in dark curls. His mustache drooped beneath the line of his jaw. He was lean, his face a provocative mixture of confidence, contemplation, and coldness.

Just now he wore a dark suit, string tie, and ruffled white shirt. The long-barreled Colt he wore was concealed by his coat flaps.

"Game's up, Mr. Justice!" the purser called from the door to the "ballroom." That was what the ship's company insisted on calling the spacious white-walled room, although since New Orleans Justice had seen it used for nothing but the passionate running poker game the purser now called him to.

Ruff nodded, turned wistfully once more toward the silent river, and then strode toward the glare and tumult of the card room. He entered, hung his hat on the hook near the door, smoothed back his hair, and walked to the table.

The faces were the familiar ones. Updike, who was rotund and heavy-handed with cards and people; the narrow, bland-eyed George Birch; the cattle buyer from Kansas, Jim Haas; and the woman.

She was the one who held Justice's glance and returned it with clear interest. Her name was Sarah Kent, and she was a tall, blue-eyed woman with a classic figure and a fine skull. She had the look of an aristocrat; her accent was pure Virginia.

"Mr. Justice," she greeted him, and he nodded, sitting as Haas broke open a deck of cards. Updike leaned back in his chair and trimmed a new cigar. Birch's emotionless glance shuttled to Ruff's eyes, held for a moment, and then flitted away.

"Jacks or better, eagle ante," Haas said, and Ruff turned his attention to the table where neat, bright stacks of gold coins sat against the blue velvet. Smoke drifted into the air in lazy, flat spirals, and the cabin boy passed by with a tray of sandwiches and liquor.

Haas riffled the cards and dealt around. Justice arranged his hand, stayed as Birch opened, and kept the two eights Haas had given him.

Sarah kept three cards, found time for a brief, cheerful smile in Ruff's direction, and sipped at her sauterne.

"You do know that Colorado country, don't you, Mr. Justice?" she asked.

"Yes. I've seen it a time or two," he assured her.

"I thought you were from Dakota," Birch said without looking up from his cards.

"I've been there too," Ruff said mildly.

"Mr. Justice has roamed the West," Sarah said effusively. "Why, last evening he was telling me—"

"You going to bet?" Updike asked with a sigh. The fat man shifted heavily in his chair. Poker was a business with him, and he was impatient with this card-party chatter.

"Twenty," Sarah said casually.

Ruff dropped his cards onto the table. He had drawn nothing to go with the eights, and Birch, having opened, obviously had a pair of jacks or better.

"If you're still of the same mind, Sarah," Justice said, "we can talk it over again this evening."

"Oh, yes," she said, frowning briefly over her cards as she stayed with Birch and Updike for another twenty dollars. "After all, I need someone to guide me, don't I?"

"You'd do better to hire someone in Saint Jo," Birch grumbled. He looked again at Justice, taking in the long hair, the narrow features of the man, the ruffled shirt. "What do you know about this man?"

"What would I know about a guide from Saint Jo?" Sarah asked logically.

Birch grunted an answer and threw down his cards as Updike revealed his full house. "You're winning a hell of a lot," Birch said, shifting his antipathy to the big man.

"I pay attention to the game," Updike snorted.

Justice lifted an eyebrow and studied George Birch briefly. The man had been tempered by hard weather. His hands were tough and brown. Webs of fine lines were engraved around his eyes. There was tension between Ruff and the man, and Justice wasn't sure if it was because Birch disliked him or because there was something between Birch and Sarah Kent.

They acted as if they had never met before New Orleans, and yet Birch was just a little too familiar at times, a little too blunt. Yet maybe that was the way he was with women.

"Are you in?" Updike asked with irritation, and Justice slid a gold eagle into the pot, nodding.

He drew three fours this time, stayed in for a heavy opening bet from Haas. The cattle buyer's face was an open book—he was holding something solid. Ruff discarded a ten and a five, got another five and a red queen in exchange, and stayed in for one more round of betting. He was aware of Sarah's deep blue eyes on him, subtly aware of the soft signals she was sending out. He had the idea Birch was aware of them as well. The man's eyes had gone colder yet.

"Fifty more," Haas said, raising again, and Ruff folded. The telltale gleam in the cattle buyer's eyes was brighter than three fours.

Updike stayed with him. Birch folded.

"If you'll stop by my cabin after a while, Mr. Justice," Sarah was saying, "we can make the arrangements. I'll need to know what your salary will be and what provisions to purchase."

"I'll stop in," he said, "and we'll go over it in detail."

"Three aces," Haas said.

"Four deuces," Updike countered, raking in the coins with his thick white hands. Haas was beginning to sweat, and Ruff wondered if he had been playing with money meant to buy cattle.

Updike shuffled and dealt. Ruff got a trash hand. Ten high, a seven, a trey, a jack, and a five. "I'm out," he said as Haas opened—tentatively this time. The hand wasn't worth drawing to.

"Around eight?" Sarah asked. Her eyes were misted,

glittering with the candlelight. He nodded his answer. She was intriguing, this woman, and if she was who General Hightower said she was, she was also dangerous.

Birch glowered at him like a jealous lover who has just been cut out. Haas was pale, his hands trembling just slightly. Ruff felt sure that Haas could afford to lose no more.

"How many?" Updike snapped.

"Two," Haas replied. Birch also took two. Sarah folded and Updike took three.

But it was the way that he took them that caused Justice's eyes to narrow.

Hadn't that last card come off the bottom? Justice wasn't sure. He had sat in on a few card games—he preferred monte—but it wasn't a passion with him and he would have been the first to admit he wasn't the most skilled at cards. Yet that movement, almost completely shielded by Updike's huge, soft hands, had seemed to be a bottom deal.

Haas lost another thirty. Birch ordered another whiskey and Updike dealt again. Justice drew two tens and stayed with it, discarding a seven, a black nine, and a six.

Haas opened, almost fearfully, and Birch folded. Ruff kept his eyes on Updike's hands, still not sure. He drew another ten and stayed with the raise, watching the confidence grow on Haas's face. Someone should tell the man he wasn't a poker player.

"What've you got?" Updike asked blandly, and Ruff showed them the tens. Haas's face fell and Updike pursed his lips.

"Sorry," the fat man said. He spread out four sevens.

Birch yawned; Haas mopped his forehead. Sarah smiled—and Ruff Justice moved.

Updike had his hand on the gold eagles when Ruff's hand shot out and covered the big man's. Updike's eyes went suddenly hard, and the facial muscles beneath the flaccid flesh tightened.

"What the hell are you doing?"

"Give it to Haas," Ruff said. His voice was soft but cold. Updike's eyes flickered.

"What is this, a joke?" Updike asked. His laugh wasn't convincing. Ruff's hand still rested on the fat man's. When Updike tried to pull his hand away, Ruff's tightened on his wrist like a band of iron.

"It's no joke," Justice said, his face intent. "You cheated the man. Give him his money."

"By God, sir, you'll not make unfounded accusations like that!" The purser, his face lined with concern, was inching toward the table. "I've been running card games on this boat for three years!"

"Then likely you've been cheating for three years," Ruff said coldly.

"What in hell is this about, Justice?" George Birch demanded.

"This." Ruff spread out Updike's hand again. "Four sevens."

"Yes?" Birch asked impatiently. "So what?"

Ruff released Updike and turned over his own discards, revealing a fifth seven. "He got a little sloppy," Ruff said. "I guess we're comparatively easy marks."

"Damn your eyes!" Haas sputtered.

Justice looked again at Updike, expecting to see discomfort, embarrassment, anything but what he did see. The man's mask had dropped away. He was no longer an amiable, slightly excitable fat man.

His small mouth had formed into a straight line, his lips compressed until they were white, bloodless. His jaw twitched with unspoken hatred; his small eyes were glowing coals. His expression was pure animal savagery, scarcely under control. If they had been alone in that room then, Justice had no doubt, the man would have lunged at him, trying to tear his throat out, to maim and blind like a wild, vengeful thing. It was pure hatred Updike radiated, and it prickled the back of Ruff's neck. The closest he had come to a look like that was on the moonlit night in New Mexico, up in the Jicarilla Mountains, when he had unexpectedly met a cougar on a high, narrow trail.

"Mr. Updike," the purser said sternly, "I believe we should have a talk with the captain."

Updike nodded and stood, but his eyes hadn't left those of Justice. His voice when he spoke was a dry hiss. "I'll kill you for this, you bastard. I'll kill you if it's the last thing I do."

He was led away by the purser, Haas tagging after them after a brief, mumbled thank-you to Ruff. Birch was contemplating his whiskey.

"He meant that," Birch said finally. "You've taken away the man's livelihood."

"He'll get over it," Ruff said for Sarah's benefit. Her eyes were shadowed with concern. "Card cheats expect to get caught from time to time."

Birch just shook his head, turning the whiskey glass in his hands. Justice rose and patted Sarah's hand. "It's nothing for you to worry about," Ruff told her. "I'll see you at eight. Your cabin."

She nodded and Ruff turned toward the door. She seemed reassured, but Ruff was not. The man meant business and he had let Justice glimpse, just for a minute, the terrible savagery that lay beneath his disarming surface. Ruff swept back his hair and planted his wide-brimmed white hat on his head.

"It was a damned-fool time to get involved in anything," he told himself as he strolled toward his own cabin. He had worked this all very nicely, casually meeting Sarah Kent, slowly gaining her confidence. And what if Updike had calmly pulled a gun and shot him?

That would have upset General Hightower's plan neatly.

He shrugged thoughts of Updike away. Most likely the man was now resting in the boat's brig—if it had one—and in the morning he would be behind bars in Saint Joseph. Ruff fished for the key to his cabin and went cautiously in. Nothing had been disturbed.

He locked the door behind him, pulled off his coat, and stretched out on the comfortable bed, which was covered with a pale green spread. He gazed at the ceiling and from time to time the small brass clock beside his bed, listening to the muffled river sounds.

An hour later he rose and stood examining himself in the mirror. He had just decided on a fresh shave when the insistent knocking at the door swiveled his head. Frowning, he drew the Colt from his holster and held it beside his leg as he answered the door. It was the purser, Mr. Goodbody.

"Thank God you're all right."

"Why? What's happened?"

"He got away. Mr. Updike. Clean away."

"How in . . . !" Ruff snapped his jaw shut and shook his head. "Let me know when you've got him, will you?"

"Certainly. The captain thinks he jumped over the side, though. He broke away and there was a splash. . . ."

"Let me know," Ruff repeated.

"Yes, sir. Sorry, sir."

Ruff nodded, locked the door behind the excited purser, and holstered his pistol. Ruff glanced again at the clock, decided to forget the shave, and pulled on his coat. Updike or no Updike, he wasn't going to miss his appointment with Sarah Kent. Still, he didn't like the idea of the man lurking out there in the dark.

That business about going over the side was a little shaky. After breaking away from the purser, Updike had only to throw some heavy object overboard and conceal himself. It would be no problem at all, and if he fooled them he could ride on in to Saint Jo instead of swimming.

The only way to play it was to figure Updike was on board still and looking for Justice. He could have all he wanted, Ruff decided—after he talked to Sarah Kent. That was of prime importance. A lot depended on it.

There were still ten minutes until eight o'clock, but Ruff was developing cabin fever. Straightening and forming his hat, he turned and went out, locking the door carefully behind him.

From far forward the sounds of voices drifted. The dining room for first-class passengers was that way. A boatman armed with a rifle walked past Ruff, who asked him, "Didn't find him yet?"

"Nah. But we will if he's aboard."

Ruff nodded and strode forward as the big paddle-wheeler rolled on, splashing its stolid way up the wide river, the paddles creaking as they clawed through the black water, the steam from the twin stacks above wisping into the dark sky.

Justice was next to the mate's cabin, aft of the engine room, when the shadow moving too quickly, too silently, leaped from the shelter of the projecting boiler shield.

A shoulder barreled into Ruff's chest and a looping fist caught him flush on the jaw. Slammed back against the railing, he pawed for his Colt, had it wrenched savagely from his hand, and felt a fist drive into his ribs, knocking the breath from him.

Ruff fought back wildly, bringing up a knee which glanced off his attacker's thigh and driving a hard right into the dark blur of his face, feeling the satisfying crunch of gristle being compacted.

But it wasn't enough. A hand arced overhead, and

there was something dark, hard, and ominous clenched in it. It landed solidly over Ruff's ear, lighting the interior of his skull with colored stars and a brief, intense sheet of flame.

Then he felt his legs buckle, felt the sickness rising in his stomach. He tried to strike out, but his arms were leaden, agonizingly slow. Hands were locked around Ruff's throat, strangling, iron-fingered hands, the thumbs digging into the jugular. Ruff felt consciousness leaking away, and for a moment he let it take him.

Then his thoughts cleared starkly. He realized fully what was happening, recognized the situation for what it was. This man was killing him!

He was damned if he'd go out that way, not after a life of fighting the Sioux and Cheyenne, of warring with the Apaches. Determination brought desperate strength. Ruff clenched his fists and brought his arms up savagely, inside of his attacker's arms. The hands were torn away from around his throat, and Ruff, choking and gasping, struck out with three fierce right-hand blows. One of them landed solidly on an ear, and the man staggered backward.

But Ruff hadn't the strength to finish it, and before he could set himself he saw the truncheon again lash out, felt his skull impact with it, and moments later, felt the shove of two fisted hands against his chest moments before he fell backward over the rail and tumbled into the dark river beneath him.

He narrowly avoided the slashing paddles of the riverboat, but the shock as he met the water was nearly as bad. He had fallen from a height and it was like falling against cement. The breath was driven from him, and he had to fight through a dark web of clinging unconsciousness to force himself to the surface, where he sucked in a long, saving breath of air.

His head still rang and he had to make an effort to

stay conscious. His eyes refused to focus and the river was cold, deathly cold. His heart thumped heavily in his chest. The riverboat, he knew by the diminishing sound, was far upstream. By willing his vision to clear he finally made out its vaguely white bulk pulling away from him, disappearing around a bend in the Missouri.

Ruff tried to swim and was making a bad job of it before his befuddled brain cleared enough for him to realize he had to shed his water-logged clothes if he hoped to make it to the shore, which seemed incredibly distant.

The boots, new in New Orleans, were difficult, but he managed to get them off, letting them sink to the river bottom. He shed his pants and coat more easily, treading water all the while.

The blows to the head had knocked the stamina from Justice's body. That, combined with the cold current, made each swimming stroke an effort. His head was alive with pinpricks of red and yellow light, his chest was on fire. The river was dark, the night black. A few stars sparkled in the cloudy, moonless sky.

The current was swift, and already Ruff knew he was miles from where he had been dumped overboard. He had been swimming for a good half an hour and the dark, formless line of the riverbank seemed as distant as ever.

He rolled onto his back and swam that way for a time, taking it slowly. It was too easy to cramp up in cold water, and there was no rush now anyway. The object was only to survive long enough to crawl ashore, to rest, to sleep.

It was another interminable period before he could do just that.

He reached the bank at a spot where the rushes grew in tangled profusion and the footing was sloppy. He staggered through the reeds and cattails, fighting for each step. The mud sucked at his feet, wanting to draw him back into the river's dark clutches.

Finally he made it. Huge, dark oaks loomed overhead, and Ruff dragged himself, cold, slimy, exhausted, onto the dry, grassy bank.

He lay still against the earth, his chest hammering, his breath coming in labored gasps, his teeth chattering with the cold. After a minute he managed to drag himself farther from the water's edge, and raking up a pile of oak leaves, he burrowed into them, covering himself with this damp and ineffective blanket against the bitter cold of the night.

He stared at the trees towering overhead for a long while, and at the stars that glittered through the gaps in the foliage, and then, mercifully, he fell asleep. A deep, dreamless sleep which lasted until the first harsh red light of dawning, when he was prodded awake with a boot toe which belonged to the grim man with the shotgun in his hands.